THE WALL
(*Intimacy*)
AND OTHER STORIES

Other books of Sartre published by New Directions

Baudelaire (*Critical Study*)

Nausea (*Novel*)

JEAN-PAUL SARTRE

The Wall

(Intimacy)

AND OTHER STORIES

Translated from the French by
LLOYD ALEXANDER

A New Directions Paperbook

TWENTY-SECOND PRINTING

DEDICATED TO OLGA KOSZAKIEWICZ

CONTENTS

THE WALL
(*Intimacy*)
AND OTHER STORIES

THE WALL

They pushed us into a big white room and I began to blink
because the light hurt my eyes. Then I saw a table and four men
behind the table, civilians, looking over the papers. They had
bunched another group of prisoners in the back and we had to
cross the whole room to join them. There were several I knew
and some others who must have been foreigners. The two in
front of me were blond with round skulls; they looked alike. I
suppose they were French. The smaller one kept hitching up his
pants; nerves.

It lasted about three hours; I was dizzy and my head was
empty; but the room was well heated and I found that pleasant
enough: for the past 24 hours we hadn't stopped shivering. The
guards brought the prisoners up to the table, one after the other.
The four men asked each one his name and occupation. Most of
the time they didn't go any further—or they would simply ask a
question here and there: "Did you have anything to do with the
sabotage of munitions?" Or "Where were you the morning of
the 9th and what were you doing?" They didn't listen to the
answers or at least didn't seem to. They were quiet for a moment
and then looking straight in front of them began to write. They
asked Tom if it were true he was in the International Brigade;
Tom couldn't tell them otherwise because of the papers they
found in his coat. They didn't ask Juan anything but they wrote
for a long time after he told them his name.

"My brother José is the anarchist," Juan said, "you know he
isn't here any more. I don't belong to any party, I never had
anything to do with politics."

They didn't answer. Juan went on, "I haven't done anything.
I don't want to pay for somebody else."

His lips trembled. A guard shut him up and took him away.
It was my turn.

"Your name is Pablo Ibbieta?"

"Yes."

The man looked at the papers and asked me, "Where's Ramon Gris?"

"I don't know."

"You hid him in your house from the 6th to the 19th."

"No."

They wrote for a minute and then the guards took me out. In the corridor Tom and Juan were waiting between two guards. We started walking. Tom asked one of the guards, "So?"

"So what?" the guard said.

"Was that the cross-examination or the sentence?"

"Sentence," the guard said.

"What are they going to do with us?"

The guard answered dryly, "Sentence will be read in your cell."

As a matter of fact, our cell was one of the hospital cellars. It was terrifically cold there because of the drafts. We shivered all night and it wasn't much better during the day. I had spent the previous five days in a cell in a monastery, a sort of hole in the wall that must have dated from the middle ages: since there were a lot of prisoners and not much room, they locked us up anywhere. I didn't miss my cell; I hadn't suffered too much from the cold but I was alone; after a long time it gets irritating. In the cellar I had company. Juan hardly ever spoke: he was afraid and he was too young to have anything to say. But Tom was a good talker and he knew Spanish well.

There was a bench in the cellar and four mats. When they took us back we sat and waited in silence. After a long moment, Tom said, "We're screwed."

"I think so too," I said, "but I don't think they'll do anything to the kid."

"They don't have a thing against him," said Tom. "He's the brother of a militiaman and that's all."

I looked at Juan: he didn't seem to hear. Tom went on, "You know what they do in Saragossa? They lay the men down on the road and run over them with trucks. A Moroccan deserter told us that. They said it was to save ammunition."

"It doesn't save gas," I said.

I was annoyed at Tom: he shouldn't have said that.

"Then there's officers walking along the road," he went on, "supervising it all. They stick their hands in their pockets and smoke cigarettes. You think they finish off the guys? Hell no.

They let them scream. Sometimes for an hour. The Moroccan said he damned near puked the first time."

"I don't believe they'll do that here," I said. "Unless they're really short on ammunition."

Day was coming in through four airholes and a round opening, they had made in the ceiling on the left, and you could see the sky through it. Through this hole, usually closed by a trap, they unloaded coal into the cellar. Just below the hole there was a big pile of coal dust; it had been used to heat the hospital but since the beginning of the war the patients were evacuated and the coal stayed there, unused; sometimes it even got rained on because they had forgotten to close the trap.

Tom began to shiver. "Good Jesus Christ, I'm cold," he said. "Here it goes again."

He got up and began to do exercises. At each movement his shirt opened on his chest, white and hairy. He lay on his back, raised his legs in the air and bicycled. I saw his great rump trembling. Tom was husky but he had too much fat. I thought how rifle bullets or the sharp points of bayonets would soon be sunk into this mass of tender flesh as in a lump of butter. It wouldn't have made me feel like that if he'd been thin.

I wasn't exactly cold, but I couldn't feel my arms and shoulders any more. Sometimes I had the impression I was missing something and began to look around for my coat and then suddenly remembered they hadn't given me a coat. It was rather uncomfortable. They took our clothes and gave them to their soldiers leaving us only our shirts—and those canvas pants that hospital patients wear in the middle of summer. After a while Tom got up and sat next to me, breathing heavily.

"Warmer?"

"Good Christ, no. But I'm out of wind."

Around eight o'clock in the evening a major came in with two *falangistas*. He had a sheet of paper in his hand. He asked the guard, "What are the names of those three?"

"Steinbock, Ibbieta and Mirbal," the guard said.

The major put on his eyeglasses and scanned the list: "Steinbock . . . Steinbock . . . oh yes . . . you are sentenced to death. You will be shot tomorrow morning." He went on looking. "The other two as well."

"That's not possible," Juan said. "Not me."

The major looked at him amazed. "What's your name?"

"Juan Mirbal," he said.

"Well, your name is there," said the major. "You're sentenced."

"I didn't do anything," Juan said.

The major shrugged his shoulders and turned to Tom and me.

"You're Basque?"

"Nobody is Basque."

He looked annoyed. "They told me there were three Basques. I'm not going to waste my time running after them. Then naturally you don't want a priest?"

We didn't even answer.

He said, "A Belgian doctor is coming shortly. He is authorized to spend the night with you." He made a military salute and left.

"What did I tell you," Tom said. "We get it."

"Yes," I said, "it's a rotten deal for the kid."

I said that to be decent but I didn't like the kid. His face was too thin and fear and suffering had disfigured it, twisting all his features. Three days before he was a smart sort of kid, not too bad; but now he looked like an old fairy and I thought how he'd never be young again, even if they were to let him go. It wouldn't have been too hard to have a little pity for him but pity disgusts me, or rather it horrifies me. He hadn't said anything more but he had turned grey; his face and hands were both grey. He sat down again and looked at the ground with round eyes. Tom was good hearted, he wanted to take his arm, but the kid tore himself away violently and made a face.

"Let him alone," I said in a low voice, "you can see he's going to blubber."

Tom obeyed regretfully; he would have liked to comfort the kid, it would have passed his time and he wouldn't have been tempted to think about himself. But it annoyed me: I'd never thought about death because I never had any reason to, but now the reason was here and there was nothing to do but think about it.

Tom began to talk. "So you think you've knocked guys off, do you?" he asked me. I didn't answer. He began explaining to me that he had knocked off six since the beginning of August; he didn't realize the situation and I could tell he didn't *want* to realize it. I hadn't quite realized it myself, I wondered if it hurt much, I thought of bullets, I imagined their burning hail through my body. All that was beside the real question; but I was calm: we had all night to understand. After a while Tom stopped talking and I watched him out of the corner of my eye; I saw he too had turned grey and he looked rotten; I told myself "Now it starts." It was almost dark, a dim glow filtered through the airholes and the pile of coal and made a big stain beneath the spot of sky; I could already see a star through the hole in the ceiling: the night would be pure and icy.

The door opened and two guards came in, followed by a blond man in a tan uniform. He saluted us. "I am the doctor," he said. "I have authorization to help you in these trying hours."

He had an agreeable and distinguished voice. I said, "What do you want here?"

"I am at your disposal. I shall do all I can to make your last moments less difficult."

"What did you come here for? There are others, the hospital's full of them."

"I was sent here," he answered with a vague look. "Ah! Would you like to smoke?" he added hurriedly, "I have cigarettes and even cigars."

He offered us English cigarettes and *puros*, but we refused. I looked him in the eyes and he seemed irritated. I said to him, "You aren't here on an errand of mercy. Besides, I know you. I saw you with the fascists in the barracks yard the day I was arrested."

I was going to continue, but something surprising suddenly happened to me; the presence of this doctor no longer interested me. Generally when I'm on somebody I don't let go. But the desire to talk left me completely; I shrugged and turned my eyes away. A little later I raised my head; he was watching me curiously. The guards were sitting on a mat. Pedro, the tall thin one, was twiddling his thumbs, the other shook his head from time to time to keep from falling asleep.

"Do you want a light?" Pedro suddenly asked the doctor. The other nodded "Yes": I think he was about as smart as a log, but he surely wasn't bad. Looking in his cold blue eyes it seemed to me that his only sin was lack of imagination. Pedro went out and came back with an oil lamp which he set on the corner of the bench. It gave a bad light but it was better than nothing: they had left us in the dark the night before. For a long time I watched the circle of light the lamp made on the ceiling. I was fascinated. Then suddenly I woke up, the circle of light disappeared and I felt myself crushed under an enormous weight. It was not the

5

thought of death, or fear; it was nameless. My cheeks burned and my head ached.

I shook myself and looked at my two friends. Tom had hidden his face in his hands. I could only see the fat white nape of his neck. Little Juan was the worst, his mouth was open and his nostrils trembled. The doctor went to him and put his hand on his shoulder to comfort him: but his eyes stayed cold. Then I saw the Belgian's hand drop stealthily along Juan's arm, down to the wrist. Juan paid no attention. The Belgian took his wrist between three fingers, distractedly, the same time drawing back a little and turning his back to me. But I leaned backward and saw him take a watch from his pocket and look at it for a moment, never letting go of the wrist. After a minute he let the hand fall inert and went and leaned his back against the wall, then, as if he suddenly remembered something very important which had to be jotted down on the spot, he took a notebook from his pocket and wrote a few lines. "Bastard," I thought angrily, "let him come and take my pulse. I'll shove my fist in his rotten face."

He didn't come but I felt him watching me. I raised my head and returned his look. Impersonally, he said to me, "Doesn't it seem cold to you here?" He looked cold, he was blue.

"I'm not cold," I told him.

He never took his hard eyes off me. Suddenly I understood and my hands went to my face: I was drenched in sweat. In this cellar, in the midst of winter, in the midst of drafts, I was sweating. I ran my hands through my hair, gummed together with perspiration; at the same time I saw my shirt was damp and sticking to my skin: I had been dripping for an hour and hadn't felt it. But that swine of a Belgian hadn't missed a thing; he had seen the drops rolling down my cheeks and thought: this is the manifestation of an almost pathological state of terror; and he had felt normal and proud of being alive because he was cold. I wanted to stand up and smash his face but no sooner had I made the slightest gesture than my rage and shame were wiped out; I fell back on the bench with indifference.

I satisfied myself by rubbing my neck with my handkerchief because now I felt the sweat dropping from my hair onto my neck and it was unpleasant. I soon gave up rubbing, it was useless; my handkerchief was already soaked and I was still sweating. My buttocks were sweating too and my damp trousers were glued to the bench.

Suddenly Juan spoke. "You're a doctor?"

"Yes," the Belgian said.

"Does it hurt . . . very long?"

"Huh? When . . . ? Oh, no," the Belgian said paternally. "Not at all. It's over quickly." He acted as though he were calming a cash customer.

"But I . . . they told me . . . sometimes they have to fire twice."

"Sometimes," the Belgian said, nodding. "It may happen that the first volley reaches no vital organs."

"Then they have to reload their rifles and aim all over again?" He thought for a moment and then added hoarsely, "That takes time!"

He had a terrible fear of suffering, it was all he thought about: it was his age. I never thought much about it and it wasn't fear of suffering that made me sweat.

I got up and walked to the pile of coal dust. Tom jumped up and threw me a hateful look: I had annoyed him because my shoes squeaked. I wondered if my face looked as frightened as his: I saw he was sweating too. The sky was superb, no light filtered into the dark corner and I had only to raise my head to see the Big Dipper. But it wasn't like it had been: the night before I could see a great piece of sky from my monastery cell and each hour of the day brought me a different memory. Morning, when the sky was a hard, light blue, I thought of beaches on the Atlantic; at noon I saw the sun and I remembered a bar in Seville where I drank *manzanilla* and ate olives and anchovies; afternoons I was in the shade and I thought of the deep shadow which spreads over half a bull-ring leaving the other half shimmering in sunlight; it was really hard to see the whole world reflected in the sky like that. But now I could watch the sky as much as I pleased, it no longer evoked anything in me. I liked that better. I came back and sat near Tom. A long moment passed.

Tom began speaking in a low voice. He had to talk, without that he wouldn't have been able to recognize himself in his own mind. I thought he was talking to me but he wasn't looking at me. He was undoubtedly afraid to see me as I was, grey and sweating: we were alike and worse than mirrors of each other. He watched the Belgian, the living.

"Do you understand?" he said. "I don't understand."

I began to speak in a low voice too. I watched the Belgian. "Why? What's the matter?"

"Something is going to happen to us that I can't understand."

There was a strange smell about Tom. It seemed to me I was more sensitive than usual to odors. I grinned. "You'll understand in a while."

"It isn't clear," he said obstinately. "I want to be brave but first I have to know. . . . Listen, they're going to take us into the courtyard. Good. They're going to stand up in front of us. How many?"

"I don't know. Five or eight. Not more."

"All right. There'll be eight. Someone'll holler 'aim!' and I'll see eight rifles looking at me. I'll think how I'd like to get inside the wall, I'll push against it with my back . . . with every ounce of strength I have, but the wall will stay, like in a nightmare. I can imagine all that. If you only knew how well I can imagine it."

"All right, all right!" I said, "I can imagine it too."

"It must hurt like hell. You know, they aim at the eyes and mouth to disfigure you," he added mechanically. "I can feel the wounds already; I've had pains in my head and in my neck for the past hour. Not real pains. Worse. This is what I'm going to feel tomorrow morning. And then what?"

I well understood what he meant but I didn't want to act as if I did. I had pains too, pains in my body like a crowd of tiny scars. I couldn't get used to it. But I was like him, I attached no importance to it. "After," I said, "you'll be pushing up daisies."

He began to talk to himself: he never stopped watching the Belgian. The Belgian didn't seem to be listening. I knew what he had come to do; he wasn't interested in what we thought; he came to watch our bodies, bodies dying in agony while yet alive.

"It's like a nightmare," Tom was saying. "You want to think something, you always have the impression that it's all right, that you're going to understand and then it slips, it escapes you and fades away. I tell myself there will be nothing afterwards. But I don't understand what it means. Sometimes I almost can . . . and then it fades away and I start thinking about the pains again, bullets, explosions. I'm a materialist, I swear it to you; I'm not going crazy. But something's the matter. I see my corpse; that's not hard but I'm the one who sees it, with my eyes. I've got to think . . . think that I won't see anything any more and the world will go on for the others. We aren't made to think that, Pablo. Believe me: I've already stayed up a whole night waiting for something. But this isn't the same: this will creep up behind us, Pablo, and we won't be able to prepare for it."

"Shut up," I said. "Do you want me to call a priest?"

He didn't answer. I had already noticed he had the tendency to act like a prophet and call me Pablo, speaking in a toneless voice. I didn't like that: but it seems all the Irish are that way. I had the vague impression he smelled of urine. Fundamentally, I hadn't much sympathy for Tom and I didn't see why, under the pretext of dying together, I should have any more. It would have been different with some others. With Ramon Gris, for example. But I felt alone between Tom and Juan. I liked that better, anyhow: with Ramon I might have been more deeply moved. But I was terribly hard just then and I wanted to stay hard.

He kept on chewing his words, with something like distraction. He certainly talked to keep himself from thinking. He smelled of urine like an old prostate case. Naturally, I agreed with him, I could have said everything he said: it isn't *natural* to die. And since I was going to die, nothing seemed natural to me, not this pile of coal dust, or the bench, or Pedro's ugly face. Only it didn't please me to think the same things as Tom. And I knew that, all through the night, every five minutes, we would keep on thinking things at the same time. I looked at him sideways and for the first time he seemed strange to me: he wore death on his face. My pride was wounded: for the past 24 hours I had lived next to Tom, I had listened to him, I had spoken to him and I knew we had nothing in common. And now we looked as much alike as twin brothers, simply because we were going to die together. Tom took my hand without looking at me.

"Pablo, I wonder . . . I wonder if it's really true that everything ends."

I took my hand away and said, "Look between your feet, you pig."

There was a big puddle between his feet and drops fell from his pants-leg.

"What is it?" he asked, frightened.

"You're pissing in your pants," I told him.

"It isn't true," he said furiously. "I'm not pissing. I don't feel anything."

The Belgian approached us. He asked with false solicitude, "Do you feel ill?"

Tom did not answer. The Belgian looked at the puddle and said nothing.

"I don't know what it is," Tom said ferociously. "But I'm not afraid. I swear I'm not afraid."

The Belgian did not answer. Tom got up and went to piss

in a corner. He came back buttoning his fly, and sat down without a word. The Belgian was taking notes.

All three of us watched him because he was alive. He had the motions of a living human being, the cares of a living human being; he shivered in the cellar the way the living are supposed to shiver; he had an obedient, well-fed body. The rest of us hardly felt ours—not in the same way anyhow. I wanted to feel my pants between my legs but I didn't dare; I watched the Belgian, balancing on his legs, master of his muscles, someone who could think about tomorrow. There we were, three bloodless shadows; we watched him and we sucked his life like vampires.

Finally he went over to little Juan. Did he want to feel his neck for some professional motive or was he obeying an impulse of charity? If he was acting by charity it was the only time during the whole night.

He caressed Juan's head and neck. The kid let himself be handled, his eyes never leaving him, then suddenly, he seized the hand and looked at it strangely. He held the Belgian's hand between his own two hands and there was nothing pleasant about them, two grey pincers gripping this fat and reddish hand. I suspected what was going to happen and Tom must have suspected it too: but the Belgian didn't see a thing, he smiled paternally. After a moment the kid brought the fat red hand to his mouth and tried to bite it. The Belgian pulled away quickly and stumbled back against the wall. For a second he looked at us with horror, he must have suddenly understood that we were not men like him. I began to laugh and one of the guards jumped up. The other was asleep, his wide-open eyes were blank.

I felt relaxed and over-excited at the same time. I didn't want to think any more about what would happen at dawn, at death. It made no sense. I only found words or emptiness. But as soon as I tried to think of anything else I saw rifle barrels pointing at me. Perhaps I lived through my execution twenty times; once I even thought it was for good: I must have slept a minute. They were dragging me to the wall and I was struggling; I was asking for mercy. I woke up with a start and looked at the Belgian: I was afraid I might have cried out in my sleep. But he was stroking his moustache, he hadn't noticed anything. If I had wanted to, I think I could have slept a while; I had been awake for 48 hours. I was at the end of my rope. But I didn't want to lose two hours of life: they would come to wake me up at dawn, I would follow them, stupefied with sleep and I would have croaked without so much as an "Oof!"; I didn't want that, I didn't want to die like an animal, I wanted to understand. Then I was afraid of having nightmares. I got up, walked back and forth, and, to change my ideas, I began to think about my past life. A crowd of memories came back to me pell-mell. There were good and bad ones—or at least I called them that *before*. There were faces and incidents. I saw the face of a little *novillero* who was gored in Valencia during the *Feria*, the face of one of my uncles, the face of Ramon Gris. I remembered my whole life: how I was out of work for three months in 1926, how I almost starved to death. I remembered a night I spent on a bench in Granada: I hadn't eaten for three days. I was angry, I didn't want to die That made me smile. How madly I ran after happiness, after women, after liberty. Why? I wanted to free Spain, I admired Pi y Margall, I joined the anarchist movement, I spoke in public meetings: I took everything as seriously as if I were immortal.

At that moment I felt that I had my whole life in front of me and I thought, "It's a damned lie." It was worth nothing because it was finished. I wondered how I'd been able to walk, to laugh with the girls: I wouldn't have moved so much as my little finger if I had only imagined I would die like this. My life was in front of me, shut, closed, like a bag and yet everything inside of it was unfinished. For an instant I tried to judge it. I wanted to tell myself, this is a beautiful life. But I couldn't pass judgment on it; it was only a sketch; I had spent my time counterfeiting eternity, I had understood nothing. I missed nothing: there were so many things I could have missed, the taste of *manzanilla* or the baths I took in summer in a little creek near Cadiz; but death had disenchanted everything.

The Belgian suddenly had a bright idea. "My friends," he told us, "I will undertake—if the military administration will allow it—to send a message for you, a souvenir to those who love you. . . ."

Tom mumbled, "I don't have anybody."

I said nothing. Tom waited an instant then looked at me with curiosity. "You don't have anything to say to Concha?"

"No."

I hated this tender complicity: it was my own fault, I had talked about Concha the night before, I should have controlled myself. I was with her for a year. Last night I would have given an arm to see her again for five minutes. That was why I talked about her, it was stronger than I was. Now I had no more desire

11

to see her, I had nothing more to say to her. I would not even have wanted to hold her in my arms: my body filled me with horror because it was grey and sweating—and I wasn't sure that her body didn't fill me with horror. Concha would cry when she found out I was dead, she would have no taste for life for months afterward. But I was still the one who was going to die. I thought of her soft, beautiful eyes. When she looked at me something passed from her to me. But I knew it was over: if she looked at me *now* the look would stay in her eyes, it wouldn't reach me. I was alone.

Tom was alone too but not in the same way. Sitting cross-legged, he had begun to stare at the bench with a sort of smile, he looked amazed. He put out his hand and touched the wood cautiously as if he were afraid of breaking something, then drew back his hand quickly and shuddered. If I had been Tom I wouldn't have amused myself by touching the bench; this was some more Irish nonsense, but I too found that objects had a funny look: they were more obliterated, less dense than usual. It was enough for me to look at the bench, the lamp, the pile of coal dust, to feel that I was going to die. Naturally I couldn't think clearly about my death but I saw it everywhere, on things, in the way things fell back and kept their distance, discreetly, as people who speak quietly at the bedside of a dying man. It was *his* death which Tom had just touched on the bench.

In the state I was in, if someone had come and told me I could go home quietly, that they would leave me my life whole, it would have left me cold: several hours or several years of waiting is all the same when you have lost the illusion of being eternal. I clung to nothing, in a way I was calm. But it was a horrible calm—because of my body; my body, I saw with its eyes, I heard with its ears, but it was no longer me; it sweated and trembled by itself and I didn't recognize it any more. I had to touch it and look at it to find out what was happening, as if it were the body of someone else. At times I could still feel it, I felt sinkings, and fallings, as when you're in a plane taking a nose dive, or I felt my heart beating. But that didn't reassure me. Everything that came from my body was all cockeyed. Most of the time it was quiet and I felt no more than a sort of weight, a filthy presence against me; I had the impression of being tied to an enormous vermin. Once I felt my pants and I felt they were damp; I didn't know whether it was sweat or urine, but I went to piss on the coal pile as a precaution.

The Belgian took out his watch, looked at it. He said, "It is three-thirty."

Bastard! He must have done it on purpose. Tom jumped; he hadn't noticed time was running out; night surrounded us like a shapeless, somber mass, I couldn't even remember that it had begun.

Little Juan began to cry. He wrung his hands, pleaded, "I don't want to die. I don't want to die."

He ran across the whole cellar waving his arms in the air then fell sobbing on one of the mats. Tom watched him with mournful eyes, without the slightest desire to console him. Because it wasn't worth the trouble: the kid made more noise than we did, but he was less touched: he was like a sick man who defends himself against illness by fever. It's much more serious when there isn't any fever.

He wept: I could clearly see he was pitying himself; he wasn't thinking about death. For one second, one single second, I wanted to weep myself, to weep with pity for myself. But the opposite happened: I glanced at the kid, I saw his thin sobbing shoulders and felt inhuman: I could pity neither the others nor myself. I said to myself, "I want to die cleanly."

Tom had gotten up, he placed himself just under the round opening and began to watch for daylight. I was determined to die cleanly and I only thought of that. But ever since the doctor told us the time, I felt time flying, flowing away drop by drop.

It was still dark when I heard Tom's voice: "Do you hear them?"

Men were marching in the courtyard.

"Yes."

"What the hell are they doing? They can't shoot in the dark."

After a while we heard no more. I said to Tom, "It's day."

Pedro got up, yawning, and came to blow out the lamp. He said to his buddy, "Cold as hell."

The cellar was all grey. We heard shots in the distance.

"It's starting," I told Tom. "They must do it in the court in the rear."

Tom asked the doctor for a cigarette. I didn't want one; I didn't want cigarettes or alcohol. From that moment on they didn't stop firing.

"Do you realize what's happening?" Tom said.

He wanted to add something but kept quiet, watching the

door. The door opened and a lieutenant came in with four soldiers. Tom dropped his cigarette.

"Steinbock?"

Tom didn't answer. Pedro pointed him out.

"Juan Mirbal?"

"On the mat."

"Get up," the lieutenant said.

Juan did not move. Two soldiers took him under the arms and set him on his feet. But he fell as soon as they released him.

The soldiers hesitated.

"He's not the first sick one," said the lieutenant. "You two carry him; they'll fix it up down there."

He turned to Tom. "Let's go."

Tom went out between two soldiers. Two others followed, carrying the kid by the armpits. He hadn't fainted; his eyes were wide open and tears ran down his cheeks. When I wanted to go out the lieutenant stopped me.

"You Ibbieta?"

"Yes."

"You wait here; they'll come for you later."

They left. The Belgian and the two jailers left too, I was alone. I did not understand what was happening to me but I would have liked it better if they had gotten it over with right away. I heard shots at almost regular intervals; I shook with each one of them. I wanted to scream and tear out my hair. But I gritted my teeth and pushed my hands in my pockets because I wanted to stay clean.

After an hour they came to get me and led me to the first floor, to a small room that smelt of cigars and where the heat was stifling. There were two officers sitting smoking in the armchairs, papers on their knees.

"You're Ibbieta?"

"Yes."

"Where is Ramon Gris?"

"I don't know."

The one questioning me was short and fat. His eyes were hard behind his glasses. He said to me, "Come here."

I went to him. He got up and took my arms, staring at me with a look that should have pushed me into the earth. At the same time he pinched my biceps with all his might. It wasn't to hurt me, it was only a game: he wanted to dominate me. He also thought he had to blow his stinking breath square in my face. We stayed for a moment like that, and I almost felt like laughing. It takes a lot to intimidate a man who is going to die; it didn't work. He pushed me back violently and sat down again. He said, "It's his life against yours. You can have yours if you tell us where he is."

These men dolled up with their riding crops and boots were still going to die. A little later than I, but not too much. They busied themselves looking for names in their crumpled papers, they ran after other men to imprison or suppress them; they had opinions on the future of Spain and on other subjects. Their little activities seemed shocking and burlesqued to me; I couldn't put myself in their place, I though they were insane. The little man was still looking at me, whipping his boots with the riding crop. All his gestures were calculated to give him the look of a live and ferocious beast.

"So? You understand?"

"I don't know where Gris is," I answered. "I thought he was in Madrid."

The other officer raised his pale hand indolently. This indolence was also calculated. I saw through all their little schemes and I was stupefied to find there were men who amused themselves that way.

"You have a quarter of an hour to think it over," he said slowly. "Take him to the laundry, bring him back in fifteen minutes. If he still refuses he will be executed on the spot."

They knew what they were doing: I had passed the night in waiting; then they had made me wait an hour in the cellar while they shot Tom and Juan and now they were locking me up in the laundry; they must have prepared their game the night before. They told themselves that nerves eventually wear out and they hoped to get me that way.

They were badly mistaken. In the laundry I sat on a stool because I felt very weak and I began to think. But not about their proposition. Of course I knew where Gris was; he was hiding with his cousins, four kilometers from the city. I also knew that I would not reveal his hiding place unless they tortured me (but they didn't seem to be thinking about that). All that was perfectly regulated, definite and in no way interested me. Only I would have liked to understand the reasons for my conduct. I would rather die than give up Gris. Why? I didn't like Ramon Gris any more. My friendship for him had died a little while before dawn at the same time as my love for Concha, at the same time as my desire to live. Undoubtedly I thought highly of him: he was tough. But it was not for this reason that I consented to die in his place; his life had no more value than mine; no life had value. They were going to slap a man up against a wall and shoot at him till he died, whether it was I or Gris or somebody else made no difference. I knew he was more useful than I to the cause of Spain but I thought to hell with Spain and anarchy; nothing was important. Yet I was there, I could save my skin and give up Gris and I refused to do it. I found that somehow comic; it was obstinacy. I thought, "I must be stubborn!" And a droll sort of gaiety spread over me.

They came for me and brought me back to the two officers. A rat ran out from under my feet and that amused me. I turned to one of the *falangistas* and said, "Did you see the rat?"

He didn't answer. He was very sober, he took himself seriously. I wanted to laugh but I held myself back because I was afraid that once I got started I wouldn't be able to stop. The *falangista* had a moustache. I said to him again, "You ought to shave off your moustache, idiot." I thought it funny that he would let the hairs of his living being invade his face. He kicked me without great conviction and I kept quiet.

"Well," said the fat officer, "have you thought about it?"

I looked at them with curiosity, as insects of a very rare species. I told them, "I know where he is. He is hidden in the cemetery. In a vault or in the gravediggers' shack."

It was a farce. I wanted to see them stand up, buckle their belts and give orders busily.

They jumped to their feet. "Let's go. Molés, go get fifteen men from Lieutenant Lopez. You," the fat man said, "I'll let you off if you're telling the truth, but it'll cost you plenty if you're making monkeys out of us."

They left in a great clatter and I waited peacefully under the guard of *falangistas*. From time to time I smiled, thinking about the spectacle they would make. I felt stunned and malicious. I imagined them lifting up tombstones, opening the doors of the vaults one by one. I represented this situation to myself as if I had been someone else: this prisoner obstinately playing the hero, these grim *falangistas* with their moustaches and their men in uniform running among the graves; it was irresistibly funny. After half an hour the little fat man came back alone. I thought he had come to give the orders to execute me. The others must have stayed in the cemetery.

The officer looked at me. He didn't look at all sheepish. "Take him into the big courtyard with the others," he said. "After the military operations a regular court will decide what happens to him."

"Then they're not . . . not going to shoot me . . . ?"

"Not now, anyway. What happens afterwards is none of my business."

I still didn't understand. I asked, "But why . . . ?"

He shrugged his shoulders without answering and the soldiers took me away. In the big courtyard there were about a hundred prisoners, women, children and a few old men. I began walking around the central grass-plot, I was stupefied. At noon they let us eat in the mess hall. Two or three people questioned me. I must have known them, but I didn't answer: I didn't even know where I was.

Around evening they pushed about ten new prisoners into the court. I recognized Garcia, the baker. He said, "What damned luck you have! I didn't think I'd see you alive."

"They sentenced me to death," I said, "and then they changed their minds. I don't know why."

"They arrested me at two o'clock," Garcia said.

"Why?" Garcia had nothing to do with politics.

"I don't know," he said. "They arrest everybody who doesn't think the way they do. He lowered his voice. "They got Gris."

I began to tremble. "When?"

"This morning. He messed it up. He left his cousin's on Tuesday because they had an argument. There were plenty of people to hide him but he didn't want to owe anything to anybody. He said, 'I'd go and hide in Ibbieta's place, but they got him, so I'll go hide in the cemetery.'"

"In the cemetery?"

"Yes. What a fool. Of course they went by there this morning, that was sure to happen. They found him in the gravediggers' shack. He shot at them and they got him."

"In the cemetery!"

Everything began to spin and I found myself sitting on the ground: I laughed so hard I cried.

THE ROOM

Mme. Darbedat held a *rahat-loukoum* between her fingers. She brought it carefully to her lips and held her breath, afraid that the fine dust of sugar that powdered it would blow away. "Just right," she told herself. She bit quickly into its glassy flesh and a scent of stagnation filled her mouth. "Odd how illness sharpens the sensations." She began to think of mosques, of obsequious Orientals (she had been to Algeria for her honeymoon) and her pale lips started in a smile: the *rahat-loukoum* was obsequious too.

Several times she had to pass the palm of her hand over the pages of her book, for in spite of the precaution she had taken they were covered with a thin coat of white powder. Her hand made the little grains of sugar slide and roll, grating on the smooth paper: "That makes me think of Arcachon, when I used to read on the beach." She had spent the summer of 1907 at the seashore. Then she wore a big straw hat with a green ribbon; she sat close to the jetty, with a novel by Gyp or Colette Yver. The wind made swirls of sand rain down upon her knees, and from time to time she had to shake the book, holding it by the corners. It was the same sensation: only the grains of sand were dry while the small bits of sugar stuck a little to the ends of her fingers. Again she saw a band of pearl grey sky above a black sea. "Eve wasn't born yet." She felt herself all weighted down with memories and precious as a coffer of sandalwood. The name of the book she used to read suddenly came back to mind: it was called *Petite Madame*, not at all boring. But ever since an unknown illness had confined her to her room she preferred memories and historical works.

She hoped that suffering, heavy readings, a vigilant attention to her memories and the most exquisite sensations would ripen her as a lovely hothouse fruit.

She thought, with some annoyance, that her husband would soon be knocking at her door. On other days of the week he came only in the evening, kissed her brow in silence and read *Le*

Temps, sitting in the armchair across from her. But Thursday was Darbedat's *day:* he spent an hour with his daughter, generally from three to four. Before going he stopped in to see his wife and both discussed their son-in-law with bitterness. These Thursday conversations, predictable to their slightest detail, exhausted Mme. Darbedat. M. Darbedat filled the quiet room with his presence. He never sat, but walked in circles about the room. Each of his outbursts wounded Mme. Darbedat like a glass splintering. This particular Thursday was worse than usual: at the thought that it would soon be necessary to repeat Eve's confessions to her husband, and to see his great terrifying body convulse with fury, Mme. Darbedat broke out in a sweat. She picked up a *loukoum* from the saucer, studied it for a while with hesitation, then sadly set it down: she did not like her husband to see her eating *loukoums.*

She heard a knock and started up. "Come in," she said weakly.

M. Darbedat entered on tiptoe. "I'm going to see Eve," he said, as he did every Thursday. Mme. Darbedat smiled at him. "Give her a kiss for me."

M. Darbedat did not answer and his forehead wrinkled worriedly: every Thursday at the same time, a muffled irritation mingled with the load of his digestion. "I'll stop in and see Franchot after leaving her, I wish he'd talk to her seriously and try to convince her."

He made frequent visits to Dr. Franchot. But in vain. Mme. Darbedat raised her eyebrows. Before, when she was well, she shrugged her shoulders. But since sickness had weighted down her body, she replaced the gestures which would have tired her by plays of emotion in the face: she said *yes* with her eyes, *no* with the corners of her mouth: she raised her eyebrows instead of her shoulders.

"There should be some way to take him away from her by force."

"I told you already it was impossible. And besides, the law is very poorly drawn up. Only the other day Franchot was telling me that they have a tremendous amount of trouble with the families: people who can't make up their mind, who want to keep the patient at home; the doctors' hands are tied. They can give their advice, period. That's all. He would," he went on, "have to make a public scandal or else she would have to ask to have him put away herself."

19

"And that," said Mme. Darbedat, "isn't going to happen tomorrow."

"No." He turned to the mirror and began to comb his fingers through his beard. Mme. Darbedat looked at the powerful red neck of her husband without affection.

"If she keeps on," said M. Darbedat," she'll be crazier than he is. It's terribly unhealthy. She doesn't leave his side, she only goes out to see you. She has no visitors. The air in their room is simply unbreathable. She never opens the window because Pierre doesn't want it open. As if you should ask a sick man. I believe they burn incense, some rubbish in a little pan, you'd think it was a church. Really, sometimes I wonder . . . she's got a funny look in her eyes, you know."

"I haven't noticed," Mme. Darbedat said. "I find her quite normal. She looks sad, obviously."

"She has a face like an unburied corpse. Does she sleep? Does she eat? But we aren't supposed to ask her about those things. But I should think that with a fellow like Pierre next to her, she wouldn't sleep a wink all night." He shrugged his shoulders. "What I find amazing is that we, her parents, don't have the right to protect her against herself. Understand that Pierre would be much better cared for by Franchot. There's a big park. And besides, I think," he added, smiling a little, "he'd get along much better with people of his own type. People like that are children, you have to leave them alone with each other; they form a sort of freemasonry. That's where he should have been put the first day and for his own good, I'd say. Of course it's in his own best interest."

After a moment, he added, "I tell you I don't like to know she's alone with Pierre, especially at night. Suppose something happened. Pierre has a very sly way about him."

"I don't know," Mme. Darbedat said, "if there's any reason to worry. He always looked like that. He always seemed to be making fun of the world. Poor boy," she sighed, "to have had his pride and then come to that. He thought he was cleverer than all of us. He had a way of saying 'You're right' simply to end the argument. . . . It's a blessing for him that he can't see the state he's in."

She recalled with displeasure the long, ironic face, always turned a little to the side. During the first days of Eve's marriage, Mme. Darbedat asked nothing more than a little intimacy with her son-in-law. But he had discouraged her: he almost never spoke, he always agreed quickly and absent-mindedly.

M. Darbedat pursued his idea. "Franchot let me visit his place," he said. "It was magnificent. The patients have private rooms with leather armchairs, if you please, and day-beds. You know, they have a tennis court and they're going to build a swimming pool."

He was planted before the window, looking out, rocking a little on his bent legs. Suddenly he turned lithely on his heels, shoulders lowered, hands in his pockets. Mme. Darbedat felt she was going to start perspiring: it was the same thing every time: now he was pacing back and forth like a bear in a cage and his shoes squeaked at every step.

"Please, please, won't you sit down. You're tiring me." Hesitating, she added, "I have something important to tell you."

M. Darbedat sat in the armchair and put his hands on his knees; a slight chill ran up Mme. Darbedat's spine: the time had come, she had to speak.

"You know," she said with an embarrassed cough, "I saw Eve on Tuesday."

"Yes."

"We talked about a lot of things, she was very nice, she hasn't been so confiding for a long time. Then I questioned her a little, I got her to talk about Pierre. Well, I found out," she added, again embarrassed, "that she is *very* attached to him."

"I know that too damned well," said M. Darbedat.

He irritated Mme. Darbedat a little: she always had to explain things in such detail. Mme. Darbedat dreamed of living in the company of fine and sensitive people who would understand her slightest word.

"But I mean," she went on, "that she is attached to him *differently* than we imagined."

M. Darbedat rolled furious, anxious eyes, as he always did when he never completely grasped the sense of an allusion or something new.

"What does that all mean?"

"Charles," said Mme. Darbedat, "don't tire me. You should understand a mother has difficulty in telling certain things."

"I don't understand a damned word of anything you say," M. Darbedat said with irritation. "You can't mean. . . ."

"Yes," she said.

"They're still . . . now, still . . . ?"

21

"Yes! Yes! Yes!" she said, in three annoyed and dry little jolts.

M. Darbedat spread his arms, lowered his head and was silent.

"Charles," his wife said, worriedly, "I shouldn't have told you. But I couldn't keep it to myself."

"Our child," he said slowly. "With this madman! He doesn't even recognize her any more. He calls her Agatha. She must have lost all sense of her own dignity."

He raised his head and looked at his wife severely. "You're sure you aren't mistaken?"

"No possible doubt. Like you," she added quickly, "I couldn't believe her and I still can't. The mere idea of being touched by that wretch. . . . So . . . ," she sighed, "I suppose that's how he holds on to her."

"Do you remember what I told you," M. Darbedat said, "when he came to ask for her hand? I told you I thought he pleased Eve *too much*. You wouldn't believe me." He struck the table suddenly, blushing violently. "It's perversity! He takes her in his arms, kisses her and calls her Agatha, selling her on a lot of nonsense about flying statues and God knows what else! Without a word from her! But what in heaven's name's between those two? Let her be sorry for him, let her put him in a sanitorium and see him every day—fine. But I never thought . . . I considered her a widow. Listen, Jeannette," he said gravely, "I'm going to speak frankly to you; if she had any sense, I'd rather see her take a lover!"

"Be quiet, Charles!" Mme. Darbedat cried.

M. Darbedat wearily took his hat and the cane he had left on the stool. "After what you've just told me," he concluded, "I don't have much hope left. In any case, I'll have a talk with her because it's my duty."

Mme. Darbedat wished he would go quickly.

"You know," she said to encourage him, "I think Eve is more headstrong than . . . than anything. She knows he's incurable but she's obstinate, she doesn't want to be in the wrong."

M. Darbedat stroked his beard absently.

"Headstrong? Maybe so. If you're right, she'll finally get tired of it. He's not always pleasant and he doesn't have much to say. When I say hello to him he gives me a flabby handshake and doesn't say a word. As soon as they're alone, I think they go back to his obsessions: she tells me sometimes he screams as though his throat were being cut because of his hallucinations. He sees statues. They frighten him because they buzz. He says they fly around and make fishy eyes at him."

He put on his gloves and continued, "She'll get tired of it, I'm not saying she won't. But suppose she goes crazy before that? I wish she'd go out a little, see the world: she'd meet some nice young man—well, someone like Schroeder, an engineer with Simplon, somebody with a future, she could see him a little here and there and she'd get used to the idea of making a new life for herself."

Mme. Darbedat did not answer, afraid of starting the conversation up again. Her husband bent over her.

"So," he said, "I've got to be on my way."

"Goodbye, Papa," Mme. Darbedat said, lifting her forehead up to him. "Kiss her for me and tell her for me she's a poor dear."

Once her husband had gone, Mme. Darbedat let herself drift to the bottom of her armchair and closed her eyes, exhausted. "What vitality," she thought reproachfully. As soon as she got a little strength back, she quietly stretched out her pale hand and took a *loukoum* from the saucer, groping for it without opening her eyes.

Eve lived with her husband on the sixth floor of an old building on the Rue du Bac. M. Darbedat slowly climbed the 112 steps of the stairway. He was not even out of breath when he pushed the bell. He remembered with satisfaction the words of Mlle. Dormoy: "Charles, for your age, you're simply marvelous." Never did he feel himself stronger and healthier than on Thursday, especially after these invigorating climbs.

Eve opened the door: that's right, she doesn't have a maid. No girls *can* stay with her. I can put myself in their place. He kissed her. "Hello, poor darling."

Eve greeted him with a certain coldness.

"You look a little pale," M. Darbedat said, touching her cheek. "You don't get enough exercise."

There was a moment of silence.

"Is Mama well?" Eve asked.

"Not good, not too bad. You saw her Tuesday? Well, she's just the same. Your Aunt Louise came to see her yesterday, that pleased her. She likes to have visitors, but they can't stay too long. Aunt Louise came to Paris for that mortgage business. I think I told you about it, a very odd sort of affair. She stopped in at the office to ask my advice. I told her there was only one thing to do: sell. She found a taker, by the way: Bretonnel. You remember Bretonnel. He's retired from business now."

He stopped suddenly: Eve was hardly listening. He thought sadly that nothing interested her any more. *It's like the books. Before, you had to tear them away from her. Now she doesn't even read any more.*

"How is Pierre?"

"Well," Eve said. "Do you want to see him?"

"Of course," M. Darbedat said gaily. "I'd like to pay him a little call."

He was full of compassion for this poor young man, but he could not see him without repugnance. *I detest unhealthy people.* Obviously, it was not Pierre's fault: his heredity was terribly loaded down. M. Darbedat sighed: *All the precautions are taken in vain, you find out those things too late.* No, Pierre was not responsible. But still he had always carried that fault in him; it formed the base of his character; it wasn't like cancer or tuberculosis, something you could always put aside when you wanted to judge a man as he is. His nervous grace, the subtlety which pleased Eve so much when he was courting her were the flowers of madness. *He was already mad when he married her only you couldn't tell.*

It makes you wonder, thought M. Darbedat, *where responsibility begins, or rather, where it ends.* In any case, he was always analyzing himself too much, always turned in on himself. But was it the cause or effect of his sickness? He followed his daughter through a long, dim corridor.

"This apartment is too big for you," he said. "You ought to move out."

"You say that every time, Papa," Eve answered, "but I've already told you Pierre doesn't want to leave his room."

Eve was amazing. Enough to make you wonder if she realized her husband's state. He was insane enough to be in a strait-jacket and she respected his decisions and advice as if he still had good sense.

"What I'm saying is for your own good." M. Darbedat went on, somewhat annoyed, "It seems to me that if I were a woman I'd be afraid of these badly lighted old rooms. I'd like to see you in a bright apartment, the kind they're putting up near Auteuil, three airy little rooms. They lowered the rents because they couldn't find any tenants; this would be just the time."

Eve quietly turned the doorknob and they entered the room.

M. Darbedat's throat tightened at the heavy odor of incense. The curtains were drawn. In the shadows he made out a thin neck above the back of an armchair: Pierre's back was turning. He was eating.

"Hello, Pierre," M. Darbedat said, raising his voice. "How are we today?" He drew near him: the sick man was seated in front of a small table; he looked sly.

"I see we had soft-boiled eggs," M. Darbedat said, raising his voice higher. "That's good!"

"I'm not deaf," Pierre said quietly.

Irritated, M. Darbedat turned his eyes toward Eve as his witness. But Eve gave him a hard glance and was silent. M. Darbedat realized he had hurt her. Too bad for her. It was impossible to find just the right tone for this boy. He had less sense than a child of four and Eve wanted him treated like a man. M. Darbedat could not keep himself from waiting with impatience for the moment when all this ridiculous business would be finished. Sick people always annoyed him a little—especially madmen because they were wrong. Poor Pierre, for example, was wrong all along the line, he couldn't speak a reasonable word and yet it would be useless to expect the least humility from him, or even temporary recognition of his errors.

Eve cleared away the eggshells and the cup. She put a knife and fork in front of Pierre.

"What's he going to eat now?" M. Darbedat said jovially.

"A steak."

Pierre had taken the fork and held it in the ends of his long, pale fingers. He inspected it minutely and then gave a slight laugh.

"I can't use it this time," he murmured, setting it down, "I was warned."

Eve came in and looked at the fork with passionate interest.

"Agatha," Pierre said, "give me another one."

Eve obeyed and Pierre began to eat. She had taken the suspect fork and held it tightly in her hands, her eyes never leaving it; she seemed to make a violent effort. How suspicious all their gestures and relationships are! thought M. Darbedat.

He was uneasy.

"Be careful, Pierre, take it by the middle because of the prongs."

Eve sighed and laid the fork on the serving table. M. Darbedat felt his gall rising. He did not think it well to give in to all this poor man's whims—even from Pierre's viewpoint it was pernicious. Franchot had said: "One must never enter the delirium of a madman." Instead of giving him another fork, it would have been better to have reasoned quietly and made him understand that the first was like all the others.

He went to the serving table, took the fork ostentatiously and tested the prongs with a light finger. Then he turned to Pierre. But the latter was cutting his meat peacefully: he gave his father-in-law a gentle, inexpressive glance.

"I'd like to have a little talk with you," M. Darbedat said to Eve.

She followed him docilely into the saloon. Sitting on the couch, M. Darbedat realized he had kept the fork in his hand. He threw it on the table.

"It's much better here," he said.

"I never come here."

"All right to smoke?"

"Of course, Papa," Eve said hurriedly. "Do you want a cigar?"

M. Darbedat preferred to roll a cigarette. He thought eagerly of the discussion he was about to begin. Speaking to Pierre he felt as embarrassed about his reason as a giant about his strength when playing with a child. All his qualities of clarity, sharpness, precision, turned against him; *I must confess it's somewhat the same with my poor Jeannette.* Certainly Mme. Darbedat was not insane, but this illness had . . . stultified her. Eve, on the other hand, took after her father . . . a straight, logical nature; discussion with her was a pleasure; *that's why I don't want them to ruin her.* M. Darbedat raised his eyes. Once again he wanted to see the fine intelligent features of his daughter. He was disappointed with this face; once so reasonable and transparent, there was now something clouded and opaque in it. Eve had always been beautiful. M. Darbedat noticed she was made up with great care, almost with pomp. She had blued her eyelids and put mascara on her long lashes. This violent and perfect make-up made a painful impression on her father.

"You're green beneath your rouge," he told her. "I'm afraid you're getting sick. And the way you make yourself up now! You used to be so discreet."

Eve did not answer and for an embarrassed moment M. Darbedat considered this brilliant, worn-out face beneath the heavy mass of black hair. He thought she looked like a tragedian. *I even know who she looks like. That woman . . . that Roumanian*

who played Phèdre *in French at the Mur d'Orange.* He regretted
having made so disagreeable a remark: *It escaped me! Better not
worry her with little things.*

"Excuse me," he said smiling, "you know I'm an old purist.
I don't like all these creams and paints women stick on their face
today. But I'm in the wrong. You must live in your time."

Eve smiled amiably at him. M. Darbedat lit a cigarette and
drew several puffs.

"My child," he began, "I wanted to talk with you: the two
of us are going to talk the way we used to. Come, sit down and
listen to me nicely; you must have confidence in your old Papa."

"I'd rather stand," Eve said. "What did you want to tell me?"

"I am going to ask you a single question," M. Darbedat said
a little more dryly. "Where will all this lead you?"

"All this?" Eve asked astonished.

"Yes . . . all this whole life you've made for yourself. Listen,"
he went on, "don't think I don't understand you" (he had a sudden illumination) "but what you want to do is beyond human
strength. You want to live solely by imagination, isn't that it?
You don't want to admit he's sick. You don't want to see the Pierre
of today, do you? You have eyes only for the Pierre of before.
My dear, my darling little girl, it's an impossible bet to win,"
M. Darbedat continued. "Now I'm going to tell you a story which
perhaps you don't know. When we were at Sables-d'Olonne—
you were three years old—your mother made the acquaintance of
a charming young woman with a superb little boy. You played
on the beach with this little boy, you were thick as thieves, you
were engaged to marry him. A while later, in Paris, your mother
wanted to see this young woman again; she was told she had had
a terrible accident. That fine little boy's head was cut off by a
car. They told your mother, 'Go and see her, but above all don't
talk to her about the death of her child, she *will not* believe he is
dead.' Your mother went, she found a half-mad creature: she lived
as though her boy was still alive; she spoke to him, she set his
place at the table. She lived in such a state of nervous tension that
after six months they had to take her away by force to a sanitorium where she was obliged to stay three years. No, my child,"
M. Darbedat said, shaking his head, "these things are impossible.
It would have been better if she had recognized the truth courage-
ously. She would have suffered once, then time would have erased
with its sponge. There is nothing like looking things in the face,
believe me."

"You're wrong," Eve said with effort. "I know very well that Pierre is. . . ."

The word did not escape. She held herself very straight and put her hands on the back of the armchair: there was something dry and ugly in the lower part of her face.

"So . . . ?" asked M. Darbedat, astonished.

"So . . . ?"

"You . . . ?"

"I love him as he is," said Eve rapidly and with an irritated look.

"Not true," M. Darbedat said forcefully. "It isn't true: you don't love him, you can't love him. You can only feel that way about a healthy, normal person. You pity Pierre, I don't doubt it, and surely you have the memory of three years of happiness he gave you. But don't tell me you love him. I won't believe you."

Eve remained wordless, staring at the carpet absently.

"You could at least answer me," M. Darbedat said coldly. "Don't think this conversation has been any less painful for me than it has for you."

"More than you think."

"Well then, if you love him," he cried, exasperated, "it is a great misfortune for you, for me and for your poor mother because I'm going to tell you something I would rather have hidden from you: before three years Pierre will be sunk in complete dementia, he'll be like a beast."

He watched his daughter with hard eyes: he was angry at her for having compelled him, by stubbornness, to make this painful revelation.

Eve was motionless; she did not so much as raise her eyes. "I knew."

"Who told you?" he asked stupefied.

"Franchot. I knew six months ago."

"And I told him to be careful with you," said M. Darbedat with bitterness. "Maybe it's better. But under those circumstances you must understand that it would be unpardonable to keep Pierre with you. The struggle you have undertaken is doomed to failure, his illness won't spare him. If there were something to be done, if we could save him by care, I'd say yes. But look: you're pretty, intelligent, gay, you're destroying yourself willingly and without profit. I know you've been admirable, but now it's over . . . done, you've done your duty and more; now it would be immoral to continue. We also have duties to ourselves, child. And then you aren't thinking about us. You must," he repeated, hammering the words, "send Pierre to Franchot's clinic. Leave this apartment where you've had nothing but sorrow and come home to us. If you want to be useful and ease the sufferings of someone else, you have your mother. The poor woman is cared for by nurses, she needs someone closer to her, and *she*," he added, "can appreciate what you do for her and be grateful."

There was a long silence. M. Darbedat heard Pierre singing in the next room. It was hardly a song, rather a sort of sharp, hasty recitative. M. Darbedat raised his eyes to his daughter.

"It's no, then?"

"Pierre will stay with me," she said quietly. "I get along well with him."

"By living like an animal all day long?"

Eve smiled and shot a glance at her father, strange, mocking and almost gay. *It's true*, M. Darbedat thought furiously, *that's not all they do; they sleep together.*

"You are completely mad," he said, rising.

Eve smiled sadly and murmured, as if to herself, "Not enough so."

"Not enough? I can only tell you one thing, my child. You frighten me."

He kissed her hastily and left. Going down the stairs he thought: *we should send out two strong-arm men who'd take the poor imbecile away and stick him under a shower without asking his advice on the matter.*

It was a fine autumn day, calm and without mystery; the sunlight gilded the faces of the passers-by. M. Darbedat was struck with the simplicity of the faces; some weather-beaten, others smooth, but they reflected all the happiness and care with which he was so familiar.

I know exactly what I resent in Eve, he told himself, entering the Boulevard St. Germain. *I resent her living outside the limits of human nature. Pierre is no longer a human being: in all the care and all the love she gives him she deprives human beings of a little. We don't have the right to refuse ourselves to the world; no matter what, we live in society.*

He watched the faces of the passers-by with sympathy; he loved their clear, serious looks. In these sunlit streets, in the midst of mankind, one felt secure, as in the midst of a large family.

A woman stopped in front of an open-air display counter. She was holding a little girl by the hand.

"What's that?" the little girl asked, pointing to a radio set.

"Mustn't touch," her mother said. "It's a radio; it plays music."

They stood for a moment without speaking, in ecstasy. Touched, M. Darbedat bent down to the little girl and smiled.

II

"He's gone." The door closed with a dry snap. Eve was alone in the salon. *I wish he'd die.*

She twisted her hands around the back of the armchair: she had just remembered her father's eyes. M. Darbedat was bent over Pierre with a competent air; he had said "That's good!" the way someone says when they speak to invalids. He had looked and Pierre's face had been painted in the depths of his sharp, bulging eyes. *I hate him when he looks at him because I think he sees him.*

Eve's hands slid along the armchair and she turned to the window. She was dazzled. The room was filled with sunlight, it was everywhere, in pale splotches on the rug, in the air like a blinding dust. Eve was not accustomed to this diligent, indiscreet light which darted from everywhere, scouring all the corners, rubbing the furniture like a busy housewife and making it glisten. However, she went to the window and raised the muslin curtain which hung against the pane. Just at that moment M. Darbedat left the building; Eve suddenly caught sight of his broad shoulders. He raised his head and looked at the sky, blinking, then with the stride of a young man he walked away. *He's straining himself,* thought Eve, *soon he'll have a stitch in the side.* She hardly hated him any longer: there was so little in that head; only the tiny worry of appearing young. Yet rage took her again when she saw him turn the corner of the Boulevard St. Germain and disappear. *He's thinking about Pierre.* A little of their life had escaped from the closed room and was being dragged through the streets, in the sun, among the people. *Can they never forget about us?*

The Rue du Bac was almost deserted. An old lady crossed the street with mincing steps; three girls passed, laughing. Then men, strong, serious men carrying briefcases and talking among themselves. *Normal people,* thought Eve, astonished at finding such a powerful hatred in herself. A handsome, fleshy woman ran heavily toward an elegant gentleman. He took her in his arms and kissed her on the mouth. Eve gave a hard laugh and let the curtain fall.

Pierre sang no more but the woman on the fourth floor was playing the piano; she played a Chopin Etude. Eve felt calmer; she took a step toward Pierre's room but stopped almost immediately and leaned against the wall in anguish; each time she left the room, she was panic-stricken at the thought of going back. Yet she knew she could live nowhere else: she loved the room. She looked around it with cold curiosity as if to gain a little time: this shadowless, odorless room where she waited for her courage to return. *You'd think it was a dentist's waiting room.* Armchairs of pink silk, the divan, the tabourets were somber and discreet, a little fatherly; man's best friends. Eve imagined those grave gentlemen dressed in light suits, all like the ones she saw at the window, entering the room, continuing a conversation already begun. They did not even take time to reconnoiter, but advanced with firm step to the middle of the room; one of them, letting his hand drag behind him like a wake in passing knocked over cushions, objects on the table, and was never disturbed by their contact. And when a piece of furniture was in their way, these poised men, far from making a detour to avoid it, quietly changed its place. Finally they sat down, still plunged in their conversation, without even glancing behind them. *A living-room for normal people,* thought Eve. She stared at the knob of the closed door and anguish clutched her throat: *I must go back. I never leave him alone so long.* She would have to open the door, then stand for a moment on the threshold, trying to accustom her eyes to the shadow and the room would push her back with all its strength. Eve would have to triumph over this resistance and enter all the way into the heart of the room. Suddenly she wanted violently to see Pierre; she would have liked to make fun of M. Darbedat with him. But Pierre had no need of her; Eve could not foresee the welcome he had in store for her. Suddenly she thought with a sort of pride that she had no place anywhere. *Normal people think I belong with them. But I couldn't stay an hour among them. I need to live out there, on the other side of the wall. But they don't want me out there.*

A profound change was taking place around her. The light had grown old and greying: it was heavy, like the water in a vase of flowers that hasn't been changed since the day before. In this aged light Eve found a melancholy she had long forgotten: the melancholy of an autumn afternoon that was ending. She looked around her, hesitant, almost timid: all that was so far away: there was neither day nor night nor season nor melancholy in the room. She vaguely recalled autumns long past, autumns of her childhood, then suddenly she stiffened: she was afraid of memories.

She heard Pierre's voice. "Agatha! Where are you?"

"Coming!" she cried.

She opened the door and entered the room.

The heavy odor of incense filled her mouth and nostrils as she opened her eyes and stretched out her hands—for a long time the perfume and the gloom had meant nothing more to her than a single element, acrid and heavy, as simple, as familiar as water, air or fire—and she prudently advanced toward a pale stain which seemed to float in the fog. It was Pierre's face: Pierre's clothing (he dressed in black ever since he had been sick) melted in obscurity. Pierre had thrown back his head and closed his eyes. He was handsome. Eve looked at his long, curved lashes, then sat close to him on the low chair. *He seems to be suffering,* she thought. Little by little her eyes grew used to the darkness. The bureau emerged first, then the bed, then Pierre's personal things: scissors, the pot of glue, books, the herbarium which shed its leaves onto the rug near the armchair.

"Agatha?"

Pierre had opened his eyes. He was watching her, smiling. "You know, that fork?" he said. "I did it to frighten that fellow. There was *almost* nothing the matter with it."

Eve's apprehensions faded and she gave a light laugh. "You succeeded," she said. "You drove him completely out of his mind."

Pierre smiled. "Did you see? He played with it a long time, he held it right in his hands. The trouble is," he said, "they don't know how to take hold of things; they grab them."

"That's right," Eve said.

Pierre tapped the palm of his left hand lightly with the index of his right.

"They take with that. They reach out their fingers and when they catch hold of something they crack down on it to knock it out."

He spoke rapidly and hardly moving his lips; he looked puzzled.

"I wonder what they want," he said at last. "That fellow has already been here. Why did they send him to me? If they want to know what I'm doing all they have to do is read it on the screen, they don't even need to leave the house. They make mistakes. They have the power but they make mistakes. I never make any, that's my trump card. *Hoffka!*" he said. He shook his long hands before his forehead. "The bitch Hoffka! Paffka! Suffka! Do you want any more?"

"Is it the bell?" asked Eve.

"Yes. It's gone." He went on severely. "This fellow, he's just a subordinate. You know him, you went into the living-room with him."

Eve did not answer.

"What did he want?" asked Pierre. "He must have told you."

She hesitated an instant, then answered brutally. "He wanted you locked up."

When the truth was told quietly to Pierre he distrusted it. He had to be dealt with violently in order to daze and paralyze his suspicions. Eve preferred to brutalize him rather than lie: when she lied and he acted as if he believed it she could not avoid a very slight feeling of superiority which made her horrified at herself.

"Lock me up!" Pierre repeated ironically. "They're crazy. What can walls do to me. Maybe they think that's going to stop me. I sometimes wonder if there aren't two groups. The real one, the Negro—and then a bunch of fools trying to stick their noses in and making mistake after mistake."

He made his hand jump up from the arm of the chair and looked at it happily.

"I can get through walls. What did you tell them?" he asked, turning to Eve with curiosity.

"Not to lock you up."

He shrugged. "You shouldn't have said that. You made a mistake too . . . unless you did it on purpose. You've got to call their bluff."

He was silent! Eve lowered her head sadly: *"They grab things!" How scornfully he said that—and he was right. Do I grab things too? It doesn't do any good to watch myself, I think most of my movements annoy him. But he doesn't say anything.* Suddenly she felt as miserable as when she was fourteen and Mme. Darbedat told her: "You don't know what to do with your hands." She didn't dare make a move and just at that time she had an irresistible desire to change her position. Quietly she put her feet under the chair, barely touching the rug. She watched the lamp on the table—the lamp whose base Pierre had painted black—and the chess set. Pierre had left only the black pawns on the board. Sometimes he would get up, go to the table and take the pawns in his hands one by one. He spoke to them, called them Robots and they seemed to stir with a mute life under his fingers. When he set them down, Eve went and touched them in her turn (she always felt somewhat ridiculous about it). They had become little bits of dead wood again but something vague and incomprehensible stayed in them, something like understanding. *These are his things*, she thought. *There is nothing of mine in the room.* She had had a few pieces of furniture before; the mirror and the little inlaid dresser handed down from her grandmother and which Pierre jokingly called *"your* dresser." Pierre had carried them away with him; things showed their true face to Pierre alone. Eve could watch them for hours: they were unflaggingly stubborn and determined to deceive her, offering her nothing but their appearance—as they did to Dr. Franchot and M. Darbedat. *Yet*, she told herself with anguish, *I don't see them quite like my father. It isn't possible for me to see them exactly like him.*

She moved her knees a little: her legs felt as though they were crawling with ants. Her body was stiff and taut and hurt her; she felt it too alive, too demanding. *I would like to be invisible and stay here seeing him without his seeing me. He doesn't need me; I am useless in this room.* She turned her head slightly and looked at the wall above Pierre. Threats were written on the wall. Eve knew it but she could not read them. She often watched the big red roses on the wallpaper until they began to dance before her eyes. The roses flamed in shadow. Most of the time the threat was written near the ceiling, a little to the left of the bed; but sometimes it moved. *I must get up. I can't . . . I can't sit down any longer.* There were also white discs on the wall that looked like slices of onion. The discs spun and Eve's hands began to tremble: *Sometimes I think I'm going mad. But no*, she thought, *I can't go mad. I get nervous, that's all.*

Suddenly she felt Pierre's hand on hers.

"Agatha," Pierre said tenderly.

He smiled at her but he held her hand by the ends of his fingers with a sort of revulsion, as though he had picked up a crab by the back and wanted to avoid its claws.

"Agatha," he said, "I would so much like to have confidence in you."

She closed her eyes and her breast heaved. *I mustn't answer anything, if I do he'll get angry, he won't say anything more.*

Pierre had dropped her hand. "I like you, Agatha," he said, "but I can't understand you. Why do you stay in the room all the time?"

Eve did not answer.

"Tell me why."

"You know I love you," she said dryly.

"I don't believe you," Pierre said. "Why should you love me? I must frighten you: I'm haunted." He smiled but suddenly became serious. "There is a wall between you and me. I see you, I speak to you, but you're on the other side. What keeps us from loving? I think it was easier before. In Hamburg."

"Yes," Eve said sadly. Always Hamburg. He never spoke of their real past. Neither Eve nor he had ever been to Hamburg.

"We used to walk along the canal. There was a barge, remember? The barge was black; there was a dog on the deck."

He made it up as he went along; it sounded false.

"I held your hand. You had another skin. I believed all you told me. Be quiet!" he shouted.

He listened for a moment. "They're coming," he said mournfully.

Eve jumped up. "They're coming? I thought they wouldn't ever come again."

Pierre had been calmer for the past three days; the statues did not come. Pierre was terribly afraid of the statues even though he would never admit it. Eve was not afraid: but when they began to fly, buzzing, around the room, she was afraid of Pierre.

"Give me the ziuthre," Pierre said.

Eve got up and took the ziuthre: it was a collection of pieces of cardboard Pierre had glued together; he used it to conjure the statues. The ziuthre looked like a spider. On one of the cardboards Pierre had written, "Power over ambush," and on the other, "Black." On a third he had drawn a laughing face with wrinkled eyes: it was Voltaire.

Pierre seized the ziuthre by one end and looked at it darkly.

"I can't use it any more," he said.

"Why?"

"They turned it upside down."

"Will you make another?"

He looked at her for a long while. "You'd like me to, wouldn't you," he said between his teeth.

Eve was angry at Pierre. *He's warned every time they come: how does he do it? He's never wrong.*

The ziuthre dangled pitifully from the ends of Pierre's fingers. *He always finds a good reason not to use it. Sunday when they came he pretended he'd lost it but I saw it behind the paste pot and he couldn't fail to see it. I wonder if he isn't the one who brings them.* One could never tell if he were completely sincere. Sometimes Eve had the impression that despite himself Pierre was surrounded by a swarm of unhealthy thoughts and visions. But at other times Pierre seemed to invent them. *He suffers. But how much does he* believe *in the statues and the Negro? Anyhow, I know he doesn't see the statues, he only hears them: when they pass he turns his head away; but he still says he sees them; he describes them.* She remembered the red face of Dr. Franchot: "But my dear madame, all mentally unbalanced persons are liars; you're wasting your time if you're trying to distinguish between what they really feel and what they pretend to feel." She gave a start. *What is Franchot doing here? I don't want to start thinking like him.*

Pierre had gotten up. He went to throw the ziuthre into the wastebasket: *I want to think like you,* she murmured. He walked with tiny steps, on tiptoe, pressing his elbows against his hips so as to take up the least possible space. He came back and sat down and looked at Eve with a closed expression.

"We'll have to put up black wallpaper," he said. "There isn't enough black in this room."

He was crouched in the armchair. Sadly Eve watched his meager body, always ready to withdraw, to shrink: the arms, legs, and head looked like retractable organs. The clock struck six. The piano downstairs was silent. Eve sighed: the statues would not come right away; they had to wait for them.

"Do you want me to turn on the light?"

She would rather not wait for them in darkness.

"Do as you please," Pierre said.

Eve lit the small lamp on the bureau and a red mist filled the room. Pierre was waiting too.

He did not speak but his lips were moving, making two dark stains in the red mist. Eve loved Pierre's lips. Before, they had been moving and sensual; but they had lost their sensuality. They were wide apart, trembling a little, coming together incessantly, crushing against each other only to separate again. They were the only living things in this blank face; they looked like two frightened animals. Pierre could mutter like that for hours without a sound leaving his mouth and Eve often let herself be fascinated by this tiny, obstinate movement. *I love his mouth.* He never kissed her any more; he was horrified at contacts: at night they touched him—the hands of men, hard and dry, pinched him all over; the long-nailed hands of women caressed him. Often he went to bed with his clothes on but the hands slipped under the clothes and tugged at his shirt. Once he heard laughter and puffy lips were placed on his mouth. He never kissed Eve after that night.

"Agatha," Pierre said, "don't look at my mouth."

Eve lowered her eyes.

"I am not unaware that people can learn to read lips," he went on insolently.

His hands trembled on the arm of the chair. The index finger stretched out, tapped three times on the thumb and the other fingers curled: this was a spell. *It's going to start,* she thought. She wanted to take Pierre in her arms.

Pierre began to speak at the top of his voice in a very sophisticated tone.

"Do you remember Sao Paulo?"

No answer. Perhaps it was a trap.

"I met you there," he said, satisfied. "I took you away from a Danish sailor. We almost fought but I paid for a round of drinks and he let me take you away. All that was only a joke."

He's lying, he doesn't believe a word of what he says. He knows my name isn't Agatha. I hate him when he lies. But she saw his staring eyes and her rage melted. *He isn't lying,* she thought, *he can't stand it any more. He feels them coming; he's talking to keep from hearing them.* Pierre dug both hands into the arm of the chair. His face was pale; he was smiling.

"These meetings are often strange," he said, "but I don't believe it's by chance. I'm not asking who sent you. I know you wouldn't answer. Anyhow, you've been smart enough to bluff me."

He spoke with great difficulty, in a sharp, hurried voice. There were words he could not pronounce and which left his mouth like some soft and shapeless substance.

"You dragged me away right in the middle of the party, between the rows of black automobiles, but behind the cars there was an army with red eyes which glowed as soon as I turned my back. I think you made signs to them, all the time hanging on my arm, but I didn't see a thing. I was too absorbed by the great ceremonies of the Coronation."

He looked straight ahead, his eyes wide open. He passed his hand over his forehead very rapidly, in one spare gesture, without stopping his talking. He did not want to stop talking.

"It was the Coronation of the Republic," he said stridently, "an impressive spectacle of its kind because of all the species of animals that the colonies sent for the ceremony. You were afraid to get lost among the monkeys. I said among the monkeys," he repeated arrogantly, looking around him, "I could say *among the Negroes!* The abortions sliding under the tables, trying to pass unseen, are discovered and nailed to the spot by my Look. The password is silence. To be silent. Everything in place and attention for the entrance of the statues, that's the countersign. Tralala . . . ," he shrieked and cupped his hands to his mouth. "Tralalala, tralalalala!"

He was silent and Eve knew that the statues had come into the room. He was stiff, pale and distrustful. Eve stiffened too and both waited in silence. Someone was walking in the corridor: it was Marie the housecleaner, she had undoubtedly just arrived. Eve thought, *I have to give her money for the gas.* And then the statues began to fly; they passed between Eve and Pierre.

Pierre went "Ah!" and sank down in the armchair, folding his legs beneath him. He turned his face away; sometimes he grinned, but drops of sweat pearled his forehead. Eve could stand the sight no longer, this pale cheek, this mouth deformed by a trembling grimace; she closed her eyes. Gold threads began to dance on the red background of her eyelids; she felt old and heavy. Not far from her Pierre was breathing violently. *They're flying, they're buzzing, they're bending over him.* She felt a slight tickling, a pain in the shoulder and right side. Instinctively her body bent to the left as if to avoid some disagreeable contact, as if to let a heavy, awkward object pass. Suddenly the floor creaked and she had an insane desire to open her eyes, to look to her right, sweeping the air with her hand.

She did nothing; she kept her eyes closed and a bitter joy made her tremble: *I am afraid too,* she thought. Her entire life had taken refuge in her right side. She leaned towards Pierre without opening her eyes. The slightest effort would be enough and she would enter this tragic world for the first time. *I'm afraid of the statues,* she thought. It was a violent, blind affirmation, an incantation. She wanted to believe in their presence with all her strength. She tried to make a new sense, a sense of touch out of the anguish which paralyzed her right side. She *felt* their passage in her arm, in her side and shoulder.

The statues flew low and gently; they buzzed. Eve knew that they had an evil look and that eyelashes stuck out from the stone around their eyes; but she pictured them badly. She knew, too, that they were not quite alive but that slabs of flesh, warm scales appeared on their great bodies; the stone peeled from the ends of their fingers and their palms were eaten away. Eve could not *see* all that: she simply thought of enormous women sliding against her, solemn and grotesque, with a human look and compact heads of stone. *They are bending over Pierre*—Eve made such a violent effort that her hands began trembling—*they are bending over me.* A horrible cry suddenly chilled her. They had touched him. She opened her eyes: Pierre's head was in his hands, he was breathing heavily. Eve felt exhausted: *a game*, she thought with remorse; *it was only a game. I didn't sincerely believe it for an instant. And all that time he suffered as if it were real.*

Pierre relaxed and breathed freely. But his pupils were strangely dilated and he was perspiring.

"Did you see them?" he asked.

"I can't see them."

"Better for you. They'd frighten you," he said. "I am used to them."

Eve's hands were still shaking and the blood had rushed to her head. Pierre took a cigarette from his pocket and brought it up to his mouth. But he did not light it:

"I don't care whether I see them or not," he said, "but I don't want them to touch me: I'm afraid they'll give me pimples."

He thought for an instant, then asked, "Did you hear them?"

"Yes," Eve said, "it's like an airplane engine." (Pierre had told her this the previous Sunday.)

Pierre smiled with condescension. "You exaggerate," he said. But he was still pale. He looked at Eve's hands. "Your hands are trembling. That made quite an impression on you, my poor Agatha. But don't worry. They won't come back again before tomorrow." Eve could not speak. Her teeth were chattering and she was afraid Pierre would notice it. Pierre watched her for a long time.

"You're tremendously beautiful," he said, nodding his head. "It's too bad, too bad."

He put out his hand quickly and toyed with her ear. "My lovely devil-woman. You disturb me a little, you are too beautiful: that distracts me. If it weren't a question of recapitulation. . . ."

He stopped and looked at Eve with surprise.

"That's not the word . . . it came . . . it came," he said, smiling vaguely. "I had another on the tip of my tongue . . . but this one . . . came in its place. I forget what I was telling you."

He thought for a moment, then shook his head.

"Come," he said, "I want to sleep." He added in a childish voice, "You know, Agatha, I'm tired. I can't collect my thoughts any more."

He threw away his cigarette and looked at the rug anxiously. Eve slipped a pillow under his head.

"You can sleep too," he told her, "they won't be back."

. . . *Recapitulation.* . . .

Pierre was asleep, a candid half-smile on his face; his head was turned to one side: one might have thought he wanted to caress his cheek with his shoulder. Eve was not sleepy, she was thoughtful: *Recapitulation.* Pierre had suddenly looked stupid and the word had slipped out of his mouth, long and whitish. Pierre had stared ahead of him in astonishment, as if he had seen the word and didn't recognize it; his mouth was open, soft: something seemed broken in it. He stammered. *That's the first time it ever happened to him: he noticed it, too. He said he couldn't collect his thoughts any more.* Pierre gave a voluptuous little whimper and his hand made a vague movement. Eve watched him harshly: *how is he going to wake up?* It gnawed at her. As soon as Pierre was asleep she had to think about it. She was afraid he would wake up wild-eyed and stammering. *I'm stupid,* she thought, *it can't start before a year; Franchot said so.* But the anguish did not leave her; a year: a winter, a springtime, a summer, the beginning of another autumn. One day his features would grow confused, his jaw would hang loose, he would half open his weeping eyes. Eve bent over Pierre's hand and pressed her lips against it: *I'll kill you before that.*

EROSTRATUS

You really have to see men from above. I put out the light and went to the window: they never suspected for a moment you could watch them from up there. They're careful of their fronts, sometimes of their backs, but their whole effect is calculated for spectators of about five feet eight. Who ever thought about the shape of a derby hat seen from the seventh floor? They neglect protecting their heads and shoulders with bright colors and garish clothes, they don't know how to fight this great enemy of Humanity, the downward perspective. I leaned on the window sill and began to laugh: where was this wonderful upright stance they're so proud of: they were crushed against the sidewalk and two long legs jumped out from under their shoulders.

On a seventh floor balcony: that's where I should have spent my whole life. You have to prop up moral superiorities with material symbols or else they'll tumble. But exactly what is my superiority over men? Superiority of position, nothing more: I have placed myself above the human within me and I study it. That's why I always liked the towers of Notre-Dame, the platforms of the Eiffel Tower, the Sacré-Coeur, my seventh floor on the Rue Delambre. These are excellent symbols.

Sometimes I had to go down into the street. To the office, for example. I stifled. It's much harder to consider people as ants when you're on the same plane as they are: they *touch* you. Once I saw a dead man in the street. He had fallen on his face. They turned him over, he was bleeding. I saw his open eyes and his cockeyed look and all the blood. I said to myself, "It's nothing, it's no more touching then wet paint. They painted his nose red, that's all." But I felt a nasty softness in my legs and neck and I fainted. They took me into a drugstore, gave me a few slaps on the face and a drink. I could have killed them.

I knew they were my enemies but they didn't know it. They liked each other, they rubbed elbows; they would even have given me a hand, here and there, because they thought I was like them. But if they could have guessed the least bit of the truth, they would have beaten me. They did later, anyhow. When they got me and knew *who* I was, they gave me the works; they beat me up for two hours in the station house, they slapped me and punched me and twisted my arms, they ripped off my pants and to finish they threw my glasses on the floor and while I looked for them, on all fours, they laughed and kicked me. I always knew they'd end up beating me; I'm not strong and I can't defend myself. Some of them had been on the lookout for me for a long time: the big ones. In the street they'd bump into me to see what I'd do. I said nothing. I acted as if I didn't understand. But they still got me. I was afraid of them: it was a foreboding. But don't think I didn't have more serious reasons for hating them.

As far as that was concerned, everything went along much better starting from the day I bought a revolver. You feel strong when you assiduously carry on your person something that can explode and make a noise. I took it every Sunday, I simply put it in my pants pocket and then went out for a walk—generally along the boulevards. I felt it pulling at my pants like a crab, I felt it cold against my thigh. But little by little it got warmer with the contact of my body. I walked with a certain stiffness, I looked like a man with a hard-on, with his thing sticking out at every step. I slipped my hand in my pocket and felt the *object*. From time to time I went into a *urinoir*—even in there I had to be careful because I often had neighbors—I took out my revolver, I felt the weight of it, I looked at its black checkered butt and its trigger that looked like a half-closed eyelid. The others, the ones who saw me from the outside, thought I was pissing. But I never piss in the *urinoirs*.

One night I got the idea of shooting people. It was a Saturday evening, I had gone out to pick up Lea, a blonde who works out in front of a hotel on the Rue Montparnasse. I never had intercourse with a woman: I would have felt robbed. You get on top of them, of course, but they eat you up with their big hairy mouth and, from what I hear, they're the ones—by a long shot—who gain on the deal. I don't ask anybody for anything, but I don't give anything, either. Or else I'd have to have a cold, pious woman who would give in to me with disgust. The first Saturday of every month I went to one of the rooms in the Hotel Duquesne with Lea. She undressed and I watched her without touching her. Sometimes I went off in my pants all by myself, other times I had time to get home and finish it. That night I didn't find her.

I waited for a little while and, as I didn't see her coming, I supposed she had a cold. It was the beginning of January and it was very cold. I was desolated: I'm the imaginative kind and I had pictured to myself all the pleasure I would have gotten from the evening. On the Rue Odessa there was a brunette I had often noticed, a little ripe but firm and plump: I don't exactly despise ripe women: when they're undressed they look more naked than the others. But she didn't know anything of my wants and I was a little scared to ask her right off the bat. And then I don't care too much for new acquaintances: these women can be hiding some thug behind a door, and after, the man suddenly jumps out and takes your money. You're lucky if you get off without a beating. Still, that evening I had nerve, I decided to go back to my place, pick up the revolver and try my luck.

So when I went up to this woman, fifteen minutes later, my gun was in my pocket and I wasn't afraid of anything. Looking at her closely, she seemed rather miserable. She looked like my neighbor across the way, the wife of the police sergeant, and I was very pleased because I'd been wanting to see her naked for a long time. She dressed with the window open when the sergeant wasn't there, and I often stayed behind my curtain to catch a glimpse of her. But she always dressed in the back of the room.

There was only one free room in the Hotel Stella, on the fifth floor. We went up. The woman was fairly heavy and stopped to catch her breath after each step. I felt good: I have a wiry body, in spite of my belly, and it takes more than five floors to wind me. On the fifth floor landing, she stopped and put her right hand to her heart and breathed heavily. She had the key to the room in her left hand.

"It's a long way up," she said, trying to smile at me. Without answering, I took the key from her and opened the door. I held my revolver in my left hand, pointing straight ahead through the pocket, and I didn't let go of it until I switched the light on. The room was empty. They had a little square of green soap on the washbasin, for a one-shot. I smiled: I don't have much to do with bidets and little squares of soap. The woman was still breathing heavily behind me and that excited me. I turned; she put out her lips towards me. I pushed her away.

"Undress," I told her.

There was an upholstered armchair; I sat down and made myself comfortable. It's at times like this I wish I smoked. The woman took off her dress and stopped, looking at me distrustfully.

"What's your name?" I asked, leaning back.

"Renée."

"All right, Renée, hurry up. I'm waiting."

"You aren't going to undress?"

"Go on," I said, "don't worry about me."

She dropped her panties, then picked them up and put them carefully on top of her dress along with her brassiere.

"So you're a little lazybones, honey?" she asked me. "You want your little girl to do all the work?"

At the same time she took a step towards me, and, leaning her hands on the arm of the chair, tried heavily to kneel between my legs. I got up brusquely.

"None of that," I told her.

She looked at me with surprise.

"Well, what do you want me to do?"

"Nothing. Just walk. Walk around. I don't want any more from you."

She began to walk back and forth awkwardly. Nothing annoys women more than walking when they're naked. They don't have the habit of putting their heels down flat. The whore arched her back and let her arms hang. I was in heaven: there I was, calmly sitting in an armchair, dressed up to my neck, I had even kept my gloves on and this ripe woman had stripped herself naked at my command and was turning back and forth in front of me. She turned her head towards me, and, for appearance, smiled coquettishly.

"You think I'm pretty? You're getting an eyeful?"

"Don't worry about that."

"Say," she asked with sudden indignation, "do you think you're going to make me walk up and down like this very long?"

"Sit down."

She sat on the bed and we watched each other in silence. She had gooseflesh. I could hear the ticking of an alarm clock from the other side of the wall. Suddenly I told her:

"Spread your legs."

She hesitated a fraction of a second then obeyed. I looked between her legs and turned up my nose. Then I began to laugh so hard that tears came to my eyes. I said, simply, "Look at that!"

And I started laughing again.

She looked at me, stupefied, then blushed violently and clapped her legs shut.

"Bastard," she said between her teeth.

But I laughed louder, then she jumped up and took her brassiere from the chair.

"Hey!" I said, "it isn't over. I'm going to give you fifty francs after a while, but I want my money's worth."

She picked up her panties nervously.

"I've had enough, get it? I don't know what you want. And if you had me come up here to make a fool out of me. . . ."

Then I took out my revolver and showed it to her. She looked at me seriously and dropped the panties without a word.

"Walk," I told her, "walk around."

She walked around for another five minutes. Then I gave her my cane and made her do exercises. When I felt my drawers were wet I got up and gave her a fifty-franc note. She took it.

"So long," I added. "I don't think I tired you out very much for the money."

I went out, I left her naked in the middle of the room, the brassiere in one hand and the fifty-franc note in the other. I didn't regret the money I spent; I had dumbfounded her and it isn't easy to surprise a whore. Going down the stairs I thought, "That's what I want. To surprise them all." I was happy as a child. I had brought along the green soap and after I reached home I rubbed it under the hot water for a long time until there was nothing left of it but a thin film between my fingers and it looked like a mint candy someone had sucked on for a long time.

But that night I woke up with a start and I saw her face again, her eyes when I showed her my gun, and her fat belly that bounced up and down at every step.

What a fool, I though. And I felt bitter remorse: I should have shot her while I was at it, shot that belly full of holes. That night and three nights afterward, I dreamed of six little red holes grouped in a circle about the navel.

As a result, I never went out without my revolver. I looked at people's backs, and I imagined, from their walk, the way they would fall if I shot them. I was in the habit of hanging around the Châtelet every Sunday when the classical concerts let out. About six o'clock I heard a bell ring and the ushers came to fasten back the plate glass doors with hooks. This was the beginning: the crowd came out slowly; the people walked with floating steps, their eyes still full of dreams, their hearts still full of pretty sentiments. There were a lot of them who looked around in amazement: the street must have seemed quite strange to them. Then they smiled mysteriously: they were passing from one world to another. I was waiting for them in this other world. I slid my right hand into my pocket and gripped the gun butt with all my strength. After a while, I *saw* myself shooting them. I knocked them off like clay pipes, they fell, one after the other and the panic-stricken survivors streamed back into the theatre, breaking the glass in the doors. It was an exciting game: when it was over, my hands were trembling and I had to go to Dreher's and drink a cognac to get myself in shape.

I wouldn't have killed the women. I would have shot them in the kidneys. Or in the calves, to make them dance.

I still hadn't decided anything. But I did everything just as though my power of decision had stopped. I began with minor details. I went to practice in a shooting gallery at Denfert-Rochereau. My scores weren't tremendous, but men are bigger targets, especially when you shoot point-blank. Then I arranged my publicity. I chose a day when all my colleagues would be together in the office. On Monday morning. I was always very friendly with them, even though I had a horror of shaking their hands. They took off their gloves to greet you; they had an obscene way of undressing their hand, pulling the glove back and sliding it slowly along the fingers, unveiling the fat, wrinkled nakedness of the palm. I always kept my gloves on.

We never did much on Mondays. The typist from the commercial service came to bring us receipts. Lemercier joked pleasantly with her and when she had gone, they described her charms with a blasé competence. Then they talked about Lindbergh. They liked Lindbergh. I told them:

"I like the black heroes."

"Negroes?" Masse asked.

"No, black as in Black Magic. Lindbergh is a white hero. He doesn't interest me."

"Go see if it's easy to cross the Atlantic," Bouxin said sourly.

I told them my conception of the black hero.

"An anarchist," Lemercier said.

"No," I said quietly, "the anarchists like their own kind of men."

"Then it must be a crazy man."

But Masse, who had some education, intervened just then.

"I know your character," he said to me. "His name is Erostratus. He wanted to become famous and he couldn't find anything better to do than to burn down the temple of Ephesus, one of the seven wonders of the world."

"And what was the name of the man who built the temple?"

"I don't remember," he confessed. "I don't believe anybody knows his name."

"Really? But you remember the name of Erostratus? You see, he didn't figure things out too badly."

The conversation ended on these words, but I was quite calm. They would remember it when the time came. For myself, who, until then, had never heard of Erostratus, his story was encouraging. He had been dead for more than two thousand years and his act was still shining like a black diamond. I began to think that my destiny would be short and tragic. First it frightened me but I got used to it. If you look at it a certain way, it's terrible, but on the other hand, it gives the passing moment considerable force and beauty. I felt a strange power in my body when I went down into the street. I had my revolver on me, the thing that explodes and makes noise. But I no longer drew my assurance from that, it was from myself: I was a being like a revolver, a torpedo or a bomb. I too, one day at the end of my somber life, would explode and light the world with a flash as short and violent as magnesium. At that time I had the same dream several nights in a row. I was an anarchist. I had put myself in the path of the Tsar and I carried an infernal machine on me. At the appointed hour, the cortège passed, the bomb exploded and we were thrown into the air, myself, the Tsar, and three gold-braided officers, before the eyes of the crowd.

I now went for weeks on end without showing up at the office. I walked the boulevards in the midst of my future victims or locked myself in my room and made my plans. They fired me at the beginning of October. Then I spent my leisure working on the following letter, of which I made 102 copies:

Monsieur:

You are a famous man and your works sell by the thousands. I am going to tell you why: because you love men. You have humanism in your blood: you are lucky. You expand when you are with people; as soon as you see one of your fellows, even without knowing him, you feel sympathy for him. You have a taste for his body, for the way he is jointed, for his legs which open and close at will, and above all for his hands: it pleases you because he has five fingers on each hand and he can set his thumb against the other fingers. You are delighted when your neighbor takes a cup from the table because there is a way of taking it which is strictly human and which you have often described in your works; less supple, less rapid than that of a monkey, but is it not so much more intelligent? You also love the flesh of man, his look of being heavily wounded with re-education, seeming to re-invent walking at every step, and his famous look which even wild beasts cannot bear. So it has been easy for you to find the proper accent for speaking to man about himself: a modest, yet frenzied accent. People throw themselves greedily upon your books, they read them in a good armchair, they think of a great love, discreet and unhappy, which you bring them and that makes up for many things, for being ugly, for being cowardly, for being cuckolded, for not getting a raise on the first of January. And they say willingly of your latest book: it's a good deed.

I suppose you might be curious to know what a man can be like who does not love men. Very well, I am such a man, and I love them so little that soon I am going out and kill half a dozen of them: perhaps you might wonder why *only* half a dozen? Because my revolver has only six cartridges. A monstrosity, isn't it? And moreover, an act strictly impolitic? But I tell you I *cannot* love them. I understand very well the way you feel. But what attracts you to them disgusts me. I have seen, as you, men chewing slowly, all the while keeping an eye on everything, the left hand leafing through an economic review. Is it my fault I prefer to watch the sea-lions feeding? Man can do nothing with his face without its turning into a game of physiognomy. When he chews, keeping his mouth shut, the corners of his mouth go up and down, he looks as though he were passing incessantly from serenity to tearful surprise. You love this, I know, you call it the watchfulness of the Spirit. But it makes me sick; I don't know why; I was born like that.

If there were only a difference of taste between us I would not trouble you. But everything happens as if you had grace and I had none. I am free to like or dislike lobster Newburg, but if I do not like men I am a wretch and can find no place in the sun. They have monopolized the sense of life. I hope you will understand what I mean. For the past 33 years I have been beating against closed doors above which is written: "No entrance if not a humanist." I have had to abandon all I have undertaken; I had to choose: either it was an absurd and ill-fated attempt, or sooner or later it had to turn to their profit. I could not succeed in detaching from myself thoughts I did not expressly destine for them, in formulating them: they remained in me as slight organic movements. Even the tools I used I felt belonged to them; words, for example: I wanted *my own* words. But the ones I use have dragged through I don't know how many consciences; they arrange themselves in my head by virtue of the habits I have picked up from the others and it is not without repugnance that I use them in writing to you. But this is the last time. I say to you: love men or it is only right for them to let you sneak out of it. Well, I do not want to sneak out. Soon I am going to take my revolver, I am going down into the street and see if anybody can do anything to *them*. Goodbye, perhaps it will be you I shall meet. You will never know then with what pleasure I shall blow your brains out. If not—and this is more likely—read tomorrow's papers. There you will see that an individual named Paul Hilbert has killed, in a moment of fury, six passers-by on the Boulevard Edgar-Quinet. You know better than anyone the value of newspaper prose. You understand then that I am not "furious." I am, on the contrary, quite calm and I pray you to accept, Monsieur, the assurance of my distinguished sentiments.

Paul Hilbert

I slipped the 102 letters in 102 envelopes and on the envelopes I wrote the addresses of 102 French writers. Then I put the whole business in my table drawer along with six books of stamps.

I went out very little during the two weeks that followed. I let myself become slowly occupied by my crime. In the mirror, to which I often went to look at myself, I noticed the changes in my face with pleasure. The eyes had grown larger, they seemed to be eating up the whole face. They were black and tender behind the glasses and I rolled them like planets. The fine eyes of an artist or assassin. But I counted on changing even more profoundly after the massacre. I have seen photographs of two beautiful girls—those servants who killed and plundered their mistress. I saw their photos *before* and *after*. *Before*, their faces poised like sky flowers above piqué collars. They smelled of hygiene and appetizing honesty. A discreet curling iron had waved their hair exactly alike. And, even more reassuringly than their curled hair, their collars and their look of being at the photographer's, there was their resemblance as sisters, their well considered resemblance which immediately put the bonds of blood and natural roots of the family circle to the fore. *After,* their faces were resplendent as fire. They had the bare neck of prisoners about to be beheaded. Everywhere wrinkles, horrible wrinkles of fear and hatred, folds, holes in the flesh as though a beast with claws had walked over their faces. And those eyes, always those black, depthless eyes—like mine. Yet they did not resemble one another. Each one, in her own way, bore the memory of the common crime. "If it is enough," I told myself, "for a crime which was mostly chance, to transform these orphans' faces, what can I not hope for from a crime entirely conceived and organized by myself." It would possess me, overturning my all-too-human ugliness . . . a crime, cutting the life of him who commits it in two. There must be times when one would like to turn back, but this shining object is there behind you, barring the way. I asked only an hour to enjoy mine, to feel its crushing weight. This time, I would arrange to have everything my way: I decided to carry out the execution at the top of the Rue Odessa. I would profit by the confusion to escape, leaving them to pick up their dead. I would run, I would cross the Boulevard Edgar-Quinet and turn quickly into the Rue Delambre. I would need only 30 seconds to reach the door of my building. My pursuers would still be on the Boulevard Edgar-Quinet, they would lose my trail and it would surely take them more than an hour to find it again. I would wait for them in my room, and when I would hear the beating on the door I would re-load my revolver and shoot myself in the mouth.

I began to live more expensively; I made an arrangement with the proprietor of a restaurant on the Rue Vavin who had a tray sent up every morning and evening. The boy rang, but I didn't open, I waited a few minutes then opened the door halfway and saw full plates steaming in a long basket set on the floor.

On October 27, at six in the evening, I had only 17 and a half francs left. I took my revolver and the packet of letters and went downstairs. I took care not to close the door, so as to re-enter more rapidly once I had finished. I didn't feel well, my hands were cold and blood was rushing to my head, my eyes tickled me. I looked at the stores, the Hotel de l'Ecole, the stationer's where I buy my pencils, and I didn't recognize them. I wondered, "What street is this?" The Boulevard Montparnasse was full of people. They jostled me, pushed me, bumped me with their elbows or shoulders. I let myself be shoved around, I didn't have the strength to slip in between them. Suddenly I saw myself in the heart of this mob, horribly alone and little. How they could have hurt me if they wanted! I was afraid because of the gun in my pocket. It seemed to me they could guess it was there. They would look at me with their hard eyes and would say: "Hey there . . . hey . . . !" with happy indignation, harpooning me with their men's paws. Lynched! They would throw me above their heads and I would fall back in their arms like a marionette. I thought it wiser to put off the execution of my plan until the next day. I went to eat at the *Cupole* for 16 francs 80. I had 70 centimes left and I threw them in the gutter.

I stayed three days in my room, without eating, without sleeping. I had drawn the blinds and I didn't dare go near the window or make a light. On Monday, someone rang at my door. I held my breath and waited. After a minute they rang again. I went on tiptoe and glued my eye to the keyhole. I could only see a piece of black cloth and a button. The man rang again and then went away. I don't know who it was. At night I had refreshing visions, palm trees, running water, a purple sky above a dome. I wasn't thirsty because hour after hour I went and drank at the spigot. But I was hungry. I saw the whore again. It was in a castle I had built in Causses Noires, about 60 miles from any town. She was naked and alone with me. Threatening her with my revolver I forced her to kneel and then run on all fours; then I tied her to a pillar and after I explained at great length what I was going to do, I riddled her with bullets. These images troubled me so much that I had to satisfy myself. Afterwards, I lay motionless in the darkness, my head absolutely empty. The furniture began to creak. It was five in the morning. I would have given anything to leave the room, but I couldn't go out because of the people walking in the street.

Day came, I didn't feel hungry any more, but I began to sweat: my shirt was soaked. Outside there was sunlight. Then I thought: "He is crouched in blackness, in a closed room, for three days. He has neither eaten nor slept. They rang and He didn't open. Soon, He is going into the street and He will kill."

I frightened myself. At six o'clock in the evening hunger struck me again. I was mad with rage. I bumped into the furniture, then I turned lights on in the rooms, the kitchen, the bath-

51

room. I began to sing at the top of my voice. I washed my hands and I went out. It took me a good two minutes to put all the letters in the box. I shoved them in by tens. I must have crumpled a few envelopes. Then I followed the Boulevard Montparnasse as far as the Rue Odessa. I stopped in front of a haberdasher's window and when I saw my face I thought, "Tonight."

I posted myself at the to of the Rue Odessa, not far from the street lamp, and waited. Two women passed, arm in arm.

I was cold but I was sweating freely. After a while I saw three men come up; I let them by: I needed six. The one on the left looked at me and clicked his tongue. I turned my eyes away.

At seven-five, two groups, followed each other closely, came out onto the Boulevard Edgar-Quinet. There was a man and a woman with two children. Behind them came three old women. I took a step forward. The woman looked angry and was shaking the little boy's arm. The man drawled,

"What a little bastard he is."

My heart was beating so hard it hurt my arms. I advanced and stood in front of them, motionless. My fingers, in my pocket, were all soft around the trigger.

"Pardon," the man said, bumping into me.

I remembered I had closed the door of the apartment and that provoked me. I would have to lose precious time opening it. The people were getting further away. I turned around and followed them mechanically. But I didn't feel like shooting them any more. They were lost in the crowd on the boulevard. I leaned against the wall. I heard eight and nine o'clock strike. I repeated to myself, "Why must I kill all these people who are dead *already?*" and I wanted to laugh. A dog came and sniffed at my feet.

When the big man passed me, I jumped and followed him. I could see the fold of his red neck between his derby and the collar of his overcoat. He bounced a little in walking and breathed heavily, he looked husky. I took out my revolver: it was cold and bright, it disgusted me, I couldn't remember very well what I was supposed to do with it. Sometimes I looked at it and sometimes I looked at his neck. The fold in the neck smiled at me like a smiling, bitter mouth. I wondered if I wasn't going to throw my revolver into the sewer.

Suddenly, the man turned around and looked at me, irritated. I stepped back.

"I wanted to ask you. . . ."

He didn't seem to be listening, he was looking at my hands.
"Can you tell me how to get to the Rue de la Gaité?"

His face was thick and his lips trembled. He said nothing. He stretched out his hand. I drew back further and said:

"I'd like. . . ."

Then I *knew* I was going to start screaming. I didn't want to: I shot him three times in the belly. He fell with an idiotic look on his face, dropped to his knees and his head rolled on his left shoulder.

"Bastard," I said, "rotten bastard!"

I ran. I heard him coughing. I also heard shouts and feet clattering behind me. Somebody asked, "Is it a fight?" then right after that someone shouted, "Murder! Murder!" I didn't think these shouts concerned me. But they seemed sinister, like the sirens of the fire engines when I was a child. Sinister and slightly ridiculous. I ran as fast as my legs could carry me.

Only I had committed an unpardonable error: instead of going up the Rue Odessa to the Boulevard Edgar-Quinet, *I was running down it toward the Boulevard Montparnasse.* When I realized it, it was too late: I was already in the midst of the crowd, astonished faces turned toward me (I remember the face of a heavily rouged woman wearing a green hat with an aigrette) and I heard the fools in the Rue Odessa shouting "murder" after me. A hand took me by the shoulder. I lost my head then: I didn't want to die stifled by this mob. I shot twice. People began to scream and scatter. I ran into a café. The drinkers jumped up as I ran through but made no attempt to stop me, I crossed the whole length of the café and locked myself in the lavatory. There was still one bullet in my revolver.

A moment went by. I was out of breath and gasping. Everything was extraordinarily silent, as though the people were keeping quiet on purpose. I raised the gun to my eyes and I saw its small hole, round and black: the bullet would come out there; the powder would burn my face. I dropped my arm and waited. After a while they came; there must have been a crowd of them, judging by the scuffling on the floor. They whispered a little and then were quiet. I was still breathing heavily and I thought they must hear me breathing from the other side of the partition. Someone advanced quietly and rattled the doorknob. He must have been flattened beside the door to avoid my bullets. I still wanted to shoot—but the last bullet was for me.

"What are they waiting for?" I wondered. "If they pushed

against the door and broke it down *right away* I wouldn't have time to kill myself and they would take me alive." But they were in no hurry; they gave me all the time in the world to die. The bastards, they were afraid.

After a while, a voice said, "All right, open up. We won't hurt you."

There was silence and the same voice went on, "You know you can't get away."

I didn't answer, I was still gasping for breath. To encourage myself to shoot, I told myself, "If they get me, they're going to beat me, break my teeth, maybe put an eye out." I wanted to know if the big man was dead. Maybe I only wounded him. . . . They were getting something ready, they were dragging something heavy across the floor. I hurriedly put the barrel of the gun in my mouth, and I bit hard on it. But I couldn't shoot, I couldn't even put my finger on the trigger. Everything was dead silent.

I threw away the revolver and opened the door.

INTIMACY

Lulu slept naked because she liked to feel the sheets caressing her body and also because laundry was expensive.

In the beginning Henri protested: you shouldn't go to bed naked like that, it isn't nice, it's dirty. Anyhow, he finally followed her example, though in his case it was merely laziness; he was stiff as a poker when there was company (he admired the Swiss, particularly the Genevans: he thought them high-class because they were so wooden) but he was negligent in small matters, for example, he wasn't very clean, he didn't change his underwear often enough; when Lulu put it in the dirty laundry bag she couldn't help noticing the bottoms were yellow from rubbing between his legs. Personally, Lulu did not despise uncleanliness: it was more intimate and made such tender shadows; in the crook of the arm, for instance; she couldn't stand the English with their impersonal bodies which smelt of nothing. But she couldn't bear the negligence of her husband, because it was a way of getting himself coddled. In the morning, he was always very tender toward himself, his head full of dreams, and broad daylight, cold water, the coarse bristles of the brush made him suffer brutal injustices.

Lulu was sleeping on her back, she had thrust the great toe of her left foot into a tear in the sheet: it wasn't a tear, it was only the hem coming apart. But it annoyed her; I have to fix that tomorrow, but still she pushed against the threads so as to feel them break. Henri was not sleeping yet, but he was quiet. He often told Lulu that as soon as he closed his eyes he felt bound by tight, resistant bonds, he could not even move his little finger. A great fly caught in a spider web. Lulu loved to feel this gross, captive body against her. If he could only stay like that, paralyzed, I would take care of him, clean him like a child and sometimes I'd turn him over on his stomach and give him a spanking, and other times when his mother came to see him, I'd find some reason to uncover him, I'd pull back the sheet and his mother would see him all naked. I think she'd fall flat on her face, it must be fifteen years since she's seen him like that. Lulu passed a light hand over her husband's hip and pinched him a little in the groin. Henri muttered but did not move. Reduced to impotence. Lulu smiled; the word "impotence" always made her smile. When she still loved Henri, and when he slept, thus, she liked to imagine he had been patiently tied up by little men like the ones she had seen in a picture when she was a child and reading *Gulliver's Travels*. She often called Henri "Gulliver" and Henri liked that because it was an English name and it made her seem educated, only he would have rather had her pronounce it with the accent. God, how they annoyed me: if he wanted someone educated all he had to do was marry Jeanne Beder, she's got breasts like hunting horns but she knows five languages. When we were still at Sceaux, on Sundays, I got so annoyed with his family I read books, any book; there was always somebody who came and watched what I was reading and his little sister asked me, "Do you understand, Lucie?" The trouble is, he doesn't think I'm distinguished enough. The Swiss, yes, they're distinguished all right because his older sister married a Swiss who gave her five children and then they impress him with their mountains. I can't have a child because of my constitution, but I never thought it was distinguished, what he does, when he goes out with me, always going into the *urinoirs* and I have to look at the store windows waiting for him, what does that make me look like? and he comes out pulling at his pants and bending his legs like an old man.

Lulu took her toe out of the slit in the sheet and wiggled her feet for the pleasure of feeling herself alert next to this soft, captive flesh. She heard rumblings: a gurgling stomach, I hate it, I can never tell whether it's his stomach or mine. She closed her eyes; liquids do it. bubbling through packs of soft pipes, everybody has them, Rirette has them, I have them (I don't like to think about it, it makes my stomach hurt). He loves me, he doesn't love my bowels, if they showed him my appendix in a glass he wouldn't recognize it, he's always feeling me, but if they put the glass in his hands he wouldn't touch it, he wouldn't think, "that's hers," you ought to love all of somebody, the esophagus, the liver, the intestines. Maybe we don't love them because we aren't used to them, if we saw them the way we saw our hands and arms maybe we'd love them; the starfish must love each other better than we do. They stretch out on the beach when there's sunlight and they poke out their stomachs to get the air and everybody can see them; I wonder where we could stick ours out, through the navel. She had closed her eyes and blue circles began to turn, like a carnival; yesterday I was shooting those circles with rubber arrows and letters lit up, one at every shot and they made the name of a city, he kept me from finishing Dijon with his mania for pressing himself up behind me, I hate people to touch me from behind, I'd rather not have a back, I don't like people to do things to me when I can't see them, they can grab a handful and then you don't see their hands, you can feel them going up and down but you can't tell where they're going, they look at you with all their eyes and you don't see them, he loves that; Henri would never think of it but he, all he thinks about is getting behind me and I know he does it on purpose to touch my behind because he knows I practically die of shame because I have one, when I'm ashamed it excites him but I don't want to think about him (she was afraid) I want to think about Rirette. She thought about Rirette every evening at the same time, just at the moment when Henri began to snuffle and grunt. But there was resistance to the thought and someone else came in her place, she even caught a glimpse of crisp black hair and she thought here it comes and she shuddered because you never know what's coming, if it's the face it's all right, that can still pass, but there were nights she spent without closing her eyes because of those horrible memories coming to the surface, it's terrible when you know all of a man and especially *that*. It isn't the same thing with Henri, I can imagine him from head to foot and it touches me because he's soft with flesh that's all grey except the belly and that's pink, he says when a well built man sits down, his belly makes three folds, but he has six, only he counts by twos and he doesn't want to see the others. She felt annoyed thinking about Rirette: "Lulu, you don't know what the body of a handsome man is like." It's ridiculous, naturally I know, she means a body hard as rock, with muscles, I don't like that, and I felt soft as a caterpillar when he hugged me against him; I married Henri because he was soft, because he looked like a priest. The priests are soft as women with their cassocks and it seems they wear stockings. When I was fifteen I wanted to lift up their skirts quietly and see their men's knees and their drawers, it was so funny they had something between their legs; I would have taken the skirt in one hand and slipped the other up their legs as far as you think, it's not that I like women so much but a man's thing when it's under a skirt is so soft, like a big flower. The trouble is you can never really hold it in your hands, if it would only stay quiet, but it starts moving like an animal, it gets hard, it frightens me when it's hard and sticking up in the air, it's brutal; God, how rotten love is. I loved Henri because his little thing never got hard, never raised its head, I laughed, sometimes I embarrassed him, I wasn't any more afraid of his than of a child's; in the evening I always took his soft little thing between my fingers, he blushed and turned his head away, sighing, but it didn't move, it behaved itself in my hand, I didn't squeeze it, we always stayed like that for a long time and then he went to sleep. Then I stretched out on my back and thought about priests and pure things, about women, and I stroked my stomach first, my beautiful flat stomach, then I slid my hands down and it was pleasure; the pleasure only I know how to give myself.

The crisp hair, the hair of a Negro. And anguish in her throat like a ball. But she closed her eyes tightly and finally the ear of Rirette appeared, a small ear, all red and golden, looking like a sugar candy. Lulu had not as much pleasure as usual at the sight of it because she heard Rirette's voice at the same time. It was a sharp, precise voice which Lulu didn't like. "You *should* go away with Pierre, Lulu; it's the only intelligent thing to do." I like Rirette very much, but she annoys me a little when she acts important and gets carried away by what she says. The night before, at the *Cupole*, Rirette was bent over her with a reasonable and somewhat haggard look. "You *can't* stay with Henri, because you don't love him, it would be a crime." She doesn't lose a chance to say something bad about him, I don't think it's very nice, he's always been perfect with her; maybe I don't love him any more, but it isn't up to Rirette to tell me; everything looks so simple and easy to her: you love or you don't love any more: but I'm not simple. First I'm used to it here and then I do like him, he's my husband. I wanted to beat her, I always wanted to hurt her because she's fat. "It would be a crime." She raised her arms, I saw her armpit, I always like her better when she has bare arms. The armpit. It was half-open, you might have thought it was a mouth; Lulu saw purple wrinkled flesh beneath the curly hairs. Pierre calls her "Minerva the Plump," she doesn't like that at all, Lulu smiled because she thought of her little brother Robert who asked her one day when she had on nothing but her slip, "Why do you have hair under your arms?" and she answered, "It's a sickness." She liked to dress in front of her little brother because he made such funny remarks, and you wondered where he picked them up. He always felt her clothes and folded her dresses carefully, his hands were so deft: one day he'll be a great dressmaker. That's a charming business, I'll design the materials for him. It's odd for a little boy to want to be a dressmaker; if I had been a boy I would have wanted to be an explorer or an actor, but not a dressmaker; but he always was a dreamer, he doesn't talk enough, he sticks to his own ideas; I wanted to be a nun and take up collections in beautiful houses. My eyes feel all soft, all soft as flesh, I'm going to sleep. My lovely pale face under the stiff head-dress, I would have looked distinguished. I would have seen hundreds of dark hallways. But the maid would have turned the light on right away; then I'd have seen family portraits, bronze statues on the tables. And closets. The woman comes with a little book and a fifty-franc note "Here you are, Sister." "Thank you, madame, God bless you. Until the next time." But I wouldn't have been a real nun. In the bus, sometimes, I'd have made eyes at some fellow, first he'd be dumbfounded, then he'd follow me, telling me a lot of nonsense and I'd have a policeman lock him up. I would have kept the collection money myself. What would I have bought? *Antidote.* It's silly. My eyes are getting softer, I like that, you'd think they were soaked in water and my whole body's comfortable. The beautiful green tiara with emeralds and lapis lazuli. The tiara turned and it was a horrible bull's head, but Lulu was not afraid, she said, "Birds of Cantal. Attention." A long red river dragged across arid countrysides. Lulu thought of her meat-grinder, then of hair grease.

"It would be a crime." She jumped bolt upright in the blackness, her eyes hard. They're torturing me. "You'll come to my house, I want you all for good intentions but she who's so reasonable for other people, she ought to know I need to think it over. He said, "You'll come!" making fiery eyes at me. "You'll come into my house, I want you all for myself!" His eyes terrify me when he wants to hypnotize; he kneaded my arms; when I see him with eyes like that I always think of the hair he has on his chest. You will come, I want you all for myself; how can he say things like that? I'm not a dog.

When I sat down, I smiled at him. I had changed my powder for him and I made up my eyes because he likes that, but he didn't see a thing, he doesn't look at my face, he looks at my breasts and I wish they'd dry up, just to annoy him, even though

I don't have too much, they're so small. You will come to my villa in Nice. He said it was white with a marble staircase, that it looked out on the sea, and we'd live naked all day, it must be funny to go up a stairway when you're naked; I'd make him go up ahead of me so that he wouldn't look at me; or else I wouldn't be able to move a foot, I'd stay motionless, wishing with all my heart he'd go blind; anyhow, that would hardly change anything; when he's there I always think I'm naked. He took me by the arm, he looked wicked, he told me, "You've got me under your skin!" and I was afraid and said, "Yes"; I want to make you happy, we'll go riding in the car, in the boat, we'll go to Italy and I'll give you everything you want. But his villa is almost unfurnished and we'd have to sleep on a mattress on the floor. He wants me to sleep in his arms and I'll smell his odor; I'd like his chest because it's brown and wide, but there's a pile of hair on it, I wish men didn't have hair, his is black and soft as moss, sometimes I stroke it and sometimes I'm horrified by it, I pull back as far as possible but he hugs me against him. He'll want me to sleep in his arms, he'll hug me in his arms and I'll smell his odor; and when it's dark we'll hear the noise of the sea and he may wake me up in the middle of the night if he wants to do it: I'll never be able to sleep peacefully except when I have my sickness because, then, he'll shut up but even so it seems there are men who do it with women then and afterwards they have blood on them, blood that isn't theirs, and there must be some on the sheets, everywhere, it's disgusting, why must we have bodies?

Lulu opened her eyes, the curtains were colored red by a light coming from the street, there was a red reflection in the mirror: Lulu loved this red light and there was an armchair which made funny shadows against the window. Henri had put his pants on the arm of the chair, and his suspenders were hanging in emptiness. I have to buy him new suspenders. Oh I don't want to, I don't want to leave. He'll kiss me all day and I'll be *his*, I'll be his pleasure, he'll look at me, he'll think, "this is my pleasure, I touched her there and there and I can do it again if it pleases me." At Port-Royal. Lulu kicked her feet in the sheets, she hated Pierre when she remembered what happened at Port-Royal. She was behind the hedge, she thought he had stayed in the car, looking at the map, and suddenly she saw him, running up behind her, he looked at her. Lulu kicked Henri. He's going to wake up. But Henri said, "Humph," and didn't waken. I'd like to know a handsome young man, pure as a girl, and we wouldn't touch each other, we'd walk along the seashore and we'd hold hands, and at night we'd sleep in twin beds, we'd stay like brother and sister and talk till morning. I'd like to live with Rirette, it's so charming, women living together; she has fat, smooth shoulders; I was miserable when she was in love with Fresnel, and it worried me to think he petted her, that he passed his hands slowly over her shoulders and thighs and she sighed. I wonder what her face must look like when she's stretched out like that, all naked, under a man, feeling hands on her flesh. I wouldn't touch her for all the money in the world, I wouldn't know what to do with her, even if she wanted, even if she said, "I want it!" I wouldn't know how, but if I were invisible I'd like to be there when somebody was doing it to her and watch her face (I'd be surprised if she still looked like Minerva) and stroke her spread knees gently, her pink knees and hear her groan. Dry throated, Lulu gave a short laugh: sometimes you think about things like that. Once she pretended Pierre wanted to rape Rirette. And I helped him, I held Rirette in my arms. Yesterday. She had fire in her cheeks, we were sitting on her sofa, one against the other, her legs were pressed together, but we didn't say anything, we'll never say anything. Henri began to snore and Lulu hissed. I'm here, I can't sleep, I'm upset and he snores, the fool. If he were to take me in his arms, beg me, if he told me, "You are all mine, Lulu, I love you, don't go!" I'd make the sacrifice for him, I'd stay, yes, I'd stay with him all my life to give him pleasure.

II

Rirette sat on the terrace of the *Dôme* and ordered a glass of port. She felt weary and angry at Lulu:

And their port has a taste of cork, Lulu doesn't care because she drinks coffee, but still you can't drink coffee at aperitif time; here they drink coffee all day or café-crème because they don't have a cent, God that must annoy them, I couldn't do it, I'd chuck the whole place in the customer's faces, these people don't need to keep up with anybody. I don't know why she always meets me in Montparnasse, it would be just as close if she met me at the Café de la Paix or the Pam-Pam, and it wouldn't take me so far from my work; impossible to imagine how sad it makes me feel to see these faces all the time, as soon as I have a minute to spare, I have to come here, it's not so bad on the terrace, but inside it smells like dirty underwear and I don't like failures.

Even on the terrace I feel out of place because I'm clean, it must surprise everybody that passes to see me in the middle of these people here who don't even shave and women who look like I don't know what. They must wonder, "What's she doing there?" I know rich Americans sometimes come in the summer, but it seems they're stopping in England now, what with the government we've got, that's why the commerce-de-luxe isn't going so well, I sold a half less than last year at this same time, and I wonder how the others make out, because I'm the best salesgirl, Mme. Dubech told me so, I feel sorry for the little Yonnel girl, she doesn't know how to sell, she can't have made a cent commission this month, and when you're on your feet all day you like to relax a little in a nice place, with a little luxury and a little art and stylish help. You like to close your eyes and let yourself go and then you like to have nice soft music, it wouldn't cost so much to go dancing at the *Ambassadeurs* sometimes; but the waiters here are so impudent, you can tell they're used to handling a cheap crowd, except the little one with brown hair who serves me, he's nice; I think Lulu must like to be surrounded with all these failures, it would scare her to go into a chic place, fundamentally, she isn't sure of herself, it frightens her as soon as there's a man with good manners, she didn't like Louis; well, she ought to be comfortable here, some of them don't even have collars, with their shoddy appearance and their pipes and the way they look at you, they don't even try to hide it, you can see they don't have enough money to pay for a woman, but that isn't what's lacking in the neighborhood, it's disgusting; you'd think they're going to eat you and they couldn't even tell you nicely that they want you, to carry it off in a way to make you feel good.

The waiter came: "Did you want dry port, mademoiselle?"

"Yes, please."

He spoke again, looking friendly, "Nice weather we're having."

"Not too soon for it," Rirette said.

"That's right. You'd think winter wouldn't ever end."

He left and Rirette followed him with her eyes. "I like that waiter," she thought, he knows his place, he doesn't get familiar, but he always has something to say to me, a little special attention.

A thin, bent young man was watching her steadily; Rirette shrugged her shoulders and turned her back on him: When they want to make eyes at a woman they could at least change their underwear. I'll tell him that if he says anything to me. I wonder why she doesn't leave. She doesn't want to hurt Henri, I think that's too stupid: a woman doesn't have the right to spoil her life for some impotent. Rirette hated impotents, it was physical. She's got to leave, she decided, her happiness is at stake, I'll tell her she can't gamble with her happiness. Lulu, you don't have the right to gamble with your happiness. I won't say anything to her, it's finished, I told her a hundred times, you can't make people happy if they don't want to be. Rirette felt a great emptiness in her head, because she was so tired, she looked at the port, all sticky in the glass, like a liquid caramel and a voice in her repeated, "Happiness, happiness," and it was a beautifully grave and tender world. And she thought that if anybody had asked her opinion in the *Paris-Soir* contest she would have said it was the most beautiful word in the French language. Did anyone think of it? They said energy, courage, but that's because they were men, there should have been a woman, the women could find it, there should have been two prizes, one for men and one for women and the most beautiful name would have been Honor; one for the women and I'd have won, I'd have said Happiness. Happiness and Honor. I'll tell her, Lulu, you don't have the right to miss out on your happiness. Your Happiness, Lulu, your Happiness. Personally, I think Pierre is very nice, first, he's a real man, and besides, he's intelligent and that never spoils anything, he has money, he'd do anything for her. He's one of those men who knows how to smooth out life's little difficulties, that's nice for a woman; I like people who know how to command, it's a knack, but he knows how to speak to waiters and head waiters; they obey him, I call that a dominant personality. Maybe that's the thing that's most lacking in Henri. And then there's the question of health, with the father she had, she should take care, it's charming to be slender and light and never to be hungry or sleepy, to sleep four hours a night and run all over Paris all day selling material but it's silly, she ought to follow a sensible diet, not eat too much at one time, but more often and at regular hours. She'll see when they send her to the sanitorium for ten years.

She stared perplexedly at the clock over the Montparnasse intersection, it said 11:20. I don't understand Lulu, she's got a funny temperament, I could never find out whether she liked men or whether they disgusted her; still, she ought to be happy with Pierre, that gives her a change, anyhow, from the one she had last year, from her Rabut, *Rebut* I called him. This memory amused her but she held back her smile because the thin young man was still watching her, she caught him by surprise when she turned her head. Rabut had a face dotted with blackheads and Lulu amused herself by removing them for him, pressed on the skin with her nails: It's sickening, but it's not her fault, Lulu doesn't know what a good-looking man is, I love cute men, first, their things are so pretty, their men's shirts, their shoes, their shiny ties, it may be crude, but it's so sweet, so strong, a sweet strength, it's like the smell of English tobacco and eau de cologne and their skin when they've just shaved, it isn't . . . it isn't like a woman's skin, you'd think it was cordova leather, and their strong arms close around you and you put your head on their chest, you smell their sweet strong odor of well-groomed men, they whisper sweet words to you; they have nice things, nice rough cowhide shoes, they whisper, "Darling, dearest darling," and you feel yourself fainting; Rirette thought of Louis who left her last year and her heart tightened; A man in love with himself, with a pile of little mannerisms, a ring and gold cigarette case and full of little manias . . . but they can be rough sometimes, worse than women. The best thing would be a man about forty, someone who still took care of himself, with grey hair on the sides, brushed back, very dry, with broad shoulders, athletic, but who'd know life and who'd be good because he'd suffered. Lulu is only a kid, she's lucky to have a friend like me, because Pierre's beginning to get tired and some people would take advantage of it if they were in my place; I always tell him to be patient, and when he gets a little sweet on me I act like I'm not paying attention, I begin to talk about Lulu and I always have a good word for her, but she doesn't deserve the luck she has, she doesn't realize; I wanted her to live alone a little the way I did when Louis went away, she'd see what it was like to go back alone to her room every evening, when you've worked all day and find the room empty and dying to put your head on a shoulder. Sometimes you wonder where you find the courage to get up the next morning and go back to work and be seductive and gay and make everybody feel good when you'd rather die than keep on with that life.

The clock struck 11:30. Rirette thought of happiness, the bluebird, the bird of happiness, the rebel bird of love. She gave a start. Lulu is half an hour late, that's usual. She'll never leave her husband, she doesn't have enough will power for that. At heart, it's mainly because of respectability that she stays with

Henri: she cheats on him but so long as they call her "Madame," she doesn't think it matters. She can say anything against him she wants but you can't repeat it the next day, she'd burn up. I did everything I could and I've told her everything I had to tell her, too bad for her.

A taxi stopped in front of the *Dôme* and Lulu stepped out. She was carrying a large valise and her face was solemn.

"I left Henri," she called.

She came nearer, bent under the weight of the valise. She was smiling.

"What?" Rirette gasped, "you don't mean. . . ."

"Yes," Lulu said. "Finished, I dropped him."

Rirette was still incredulous. "He knows? You told him?"

Lulu's eyes clouded. "And how!" she said.

"Well, well . . . my own little Lulu!"

Rirette did not know what to think, but in any case, she supposed Lulu needed encouragement.

"That's good news," she said. "How brave you were."

She felt like adding: you see, it wasn't so hard. But she restrained herself. Lulu let herself be admired: she had rouged her cheeks and her eyes were bright. She sat and put the valise down near her. She was wearing a grey wool coat with a leather belt, a light yellow sweater with a rolled collar. She was bareheaded. She recognized immediately the blend of guilt and amusement she was plunged in; Lulu always made that impression on her. What I like about her, Rirette thought, is her vitality.

"In two shakes," Lulu said, "I told him what I thought. He was struck dumb."

"I can't get over it," said Rirette. "But what came over you, darling? Yesterday evening I'd have bet my last franc you'd never leave him."

"It's on account of my kid brother, I don't mind him getting stuck up with me but I can't stand it when he starts on my family."

"But how did it happen?"

"Where's the waiter?" Lulu asked, stirring restlessly on the chair. "The Dôme waiters aren't ever there when you want them. Is the little brown-haired one serving us?"

"Yes," Rirette said, "did you know he's mad about me?"

"Oh? Look out for the woman in the washroom then, he's always mixed up with her. He makes passes at her but I think he just does it to see the women go into the toilets; when they come out he looks hard enough to make you blush. By the way, I've got to leave you for a minute, I have to go down and call Pierre, I'd like to see his face! If you see the waiter, order a café-crême for me: I'll only be a minute and then I'll tell you everything."

She got up, took a few steps and came back towards Rirette. "Dearest Lulu," said Rirette, taking her by the hands.

Lulu left her and stepped lightly across the terrace. Rirette watched her. I never thought she could do it. How gay she is, she thought, a little scandalized, it's good for her to walk out on her husband. If she had listened to me she'd have done it long ago. Anyhow, it's thanks to me; fundamentally, I have a lot of influence on her.

Lulu was back a few minutes later.

"Pierre was bowled over," she said, "He wanted the details but I'll give them to him later, I'm lunching with him. He says maybe we can leave tomorrow night."

"How glad I am, Lulu," Rirette said. "Tell me quickly. Did you decide last night?"

"You know, I didn't decide anything," Lulu said modestly, "It was decided all by itself." She tapped nervously on the table. "Waiter! Waiter! God, he annoys me. I'd like a café-crême."

Rirette was shocked. In Lulu's place and under circumstances as serious as this she wouldn't have lost time running after a café-crême. Lulu was charming, but it was amazing how futile she could be, like a bird.

Lulu burst out laughing. "If you'd seen Henri's face!

"I wonder what your mother will say?" said Rirette seriously.

"My mother? She'll be en-chan-ted," Lulu said with assurance. "He was impolite with her, you know, she was fed up. Always complaining because she didn't bring me up right, that I was this, I was that, that you could see I was brought up in a barn. You know, what I did was a little because of her."

"But what happened?"

"Well, he slapped Robert."

"You mean Robert was in your place?"

"Yes, just passing by this morning because mother wants to apprentice him with Gompez. I think I told you. So, he stopped in while we were eating breakfast and Henri slapped him."

"But why?" Rirette asked, slightly annoyed. She hated the way Lulu told stories.

"They had an argument," Lulu said vaguely, "and the boy

wouldn't let himself be insulted. He stood right up to him. 'Old asshole,' he called him, right to his face. Because Henri said he was poorly raised, naturally, that's all he can say. I thought I'd die laughing. Then Henri got up, we were eating in the kitchenette, and smacked him, I could have killed him!"

"So you left?"

"Left?" Lulu asked, amazed. "Where?"

"I thought you left him then. Look, Lulu, you've got to tell me these things in order, otherwise I don't understand. Tell me," she added, suspiciously, "you really left him, that's all true?"

"Of course. I've been explaining to you for an hour."

"Good. So Henri slapped Robert. Then what?"

"Then," Lulu said, "I locked him on the balcony, it was too funny! He was still in his pajamas, tapping on the window but he didn't dare break the glass because he's as mean as dirt. If I had been in his place, I'd have broken up everything, even if I had to cut my hands to pieces. And the Texiers came in. Then he started smiling through the window acting as if it were a joke."

The waiter passed; Lulu seized his arm:

"So there you are, waiter. Would it trouble you too much to get me a café-crème?"

Rirette was annoyed and she smiled knowingly at the waiter but the waiter remained solemn and bowed with guilty obsequiousness. Rirette was a little angry at Lulu: she never knew the right tone to use on inferiors, sometimes she was too familiar, sometimes too dry and demanding.

Lulu began to laugh.

"I'm laughing because I can still see Henri in his pajamas on the balcony; he was shivering with cold. Do you know how I managed to lock him out? He was in the back of the kitchenette, Robert was crying and he was making a sermon. I opened the window and told him, 'Look, Henri! There's a taxi that just knocked over the flower woman.' He came right out; he likes the flower woman because she told him she was Swiss and he thinks she's in love with him. 'Where? Where?' he kept saying. I stepped back quietly, into the room, and closed the window. Then I shouted through the glass, 'That'll teach you to be a brute to my brother.' I left him on the balcony more than an hour, he kept watching us with big round eyes, he was green with rage. I stuck my tongue out at him and gave Robert candy; after that I brought my things into the kitchenette and got dressed in front of Robert because I know Henri hates that: Robert kissed my arms and neck like a little man, he's so charming, we acted as if Henri weren't there. On top of all that, I forgot to wash."

"And Henri outside the window. It's too funny for words," Rirette said, bursting with laughter.

Lulu stopped laughing. "I'm afraid he'll catch cold," she said seriously. "You don't think when you're mad." She went on gaily, "He shook his fist at us and kept talking all the time but I didn't understand half of what he said. Then Robert left and right after that the Texiers rang and I let them in. When he saw them he was all smiles and bowing at them and I told them, 'Look at my husband, my big darling, doesn't he look like a fish in an aquarium?' The Texiers waved at him through the glass, they were a little surprised but they didn't let on."

"I can see it all," Rirette said, laughing. "Haha! Your husband on the balcony and the Texiers in the kitchenette. . . ." She wanted to find the right comic and picturesque words to describe the scene to Lulu, she thought Lulu did not have a real sense of humor, but the words did not come.

"I opened the window," Lulu said, "and Henri came in. He kissed me in front of the Texiers and called me a little clown. 'Oh, the little clown,' he said, 'she wanted to play a trick on me.' And I smiled and the Texiers smiled politely, everybody smiled. But when they left he hit me on the ear. Then I took a brush and hit him in the corner of the mouth with it: I split his lip."

"Poor girl," Rirette said with tenderness.

But with a gesture Lulu dismissed all compassion. She held herself straight, shaking her brown curls combatively and her eyes flashed lightning.

"Then we talked it over: I washed his mouth with a towel and then I told him I was sick of it, that I didn't love him any more and that I was leaving. He began to cry. He said he'd kill himself. But that didn't work any more: you remember, Rirette, last year, when there was all that trouble in the Rhineland, he sang the same tune every day: 'There's going to be a war, I'm going to enlist and I'll be killed and you'll be sorry, you'll regret all the sorrow you've caused me.' 'That's enough,' I told him, 'you're impotent, they wouldn't take you.' Anyhow, I calmed him down because he was talking about locking me up in the kitchenette, I swore I wouldn't leave before a month. After that he went to the office, his eyes were all red and there was a piece of cloth sticking to his lip, he didn't look too good. I did the housework, I put the lentils on the stove and packed my bag. I left him a note on the kitchen table."

"What did you write?"

"I said," Lulu said proudly, "The lentils are on the stove. Help yourself and turn off the gas. There's ham in the icebox. I'm fed up and I'm leaving. Goodbye."

They both laughed and two passers-by turned around. Rirette thought they must present a charming sight and was sorry they weren't sitting on the terrace of the *Viel* or the *Café de la Paix.* When they finished laughing, they were silent a moment and Rirette realized they had nothing more to say to each other. She was a little disappointed.

"I've got to run," Lulu said, rising; "I meet Pierre at noon. What am I going to do with my bag?"

"Leave it with me," Rirette said, "I'll check it with the woman in the ladies' room. When will I see you again?"

"I'll pick you up at your place at two, I have a pile of errands to do: I didn't take half my things, Pierre's going to have to give me money."

Lulu left and Rirette called the waiter. She felt grave and sad enough for two. The waiter ran up: Rirete already noticed that he always hurried when she called him.

"That's five francs," he said. He added a little dryly, "You two were pretty gay, I could hear you laughing all the way back there."

Lulu hurt his feelings, thought Rirette, spitefully. Blushing, she said, "My friend is a little nervous this morning."

"She's very charming," the waiter said soulfully. "Thank you very much, mademoiselle."

He pocketed the six francs and went off. Rirette was a little amazed, but noon struck and she thought it was time for Henri to come back and find Lulu's note: this was a moment full of sweetness for her.

III

"I'd like all that to be sent *before tomorrow evening,* to the Hotel du Théatre, Rue Vandamme." Lulu told the cashier, putting on the air of a great lady. She turned to Rirette:

"It's all over. Let's go."

"What name?" the cashier asked.

"Mme. Lucienne Crispin."

Lulu threw her coat over her arm and began to run; she ran down the wide staircase of the Samaritain. Rirette followed her, almost falling several times because she didn't watch her step: she had eyes only for the slender silhouette of blue and canary yellow dancing before her! It's true, she does have an obscene body . . . Each time Rirette saw Lulu from behind or in profile, she was struck by the obscenity of her shape though she could not explain why; it was an impression. She's supple and slender, but there's something indecent about her, I don't know what. She does everything she can do to display herself, that must be it. She says she's ashamed of her behind and still she wears skirts that cling to her rump. Her tail is small, yes, a lot smaller than mine, but you can see more of it. It's all around, under her thin back, it fills the skirt, you'd think it was poured in, and besides it jiggles.

Lulu turned around and they smiled at each other. Rirette thought of her friend's indiscreet body with a mixture of reprobation and languor: tight little breasts, a polished flesh, all yellow —when you touched it you'd swear it was rubber—long thighs, a long, common body with long legs: the body of a Negress, Rirette thought, she looks like a Negress dancing the rumba. Near the revolving door a mirror gave Rirette the reflection of her own full body. I'm more the athletic type, she thought, taking Lulu's arm, she makes a better impression than I do when we're dressed, but naked, I'm sure I'm better than she is.

They stayed silent for a moment, then Lulu said:

"Pierre was simply charming. You've been charming too, Rirette, and I'm very grateful to both of you."

She said that with a constrained air, but Rirette paid no attention: Lulu never knew how to thank people, she was too timid.

"What a bore," Lulu said suddenly, "I have to buy a brassiere."

"Here?" Rirette asked. They were just passing a lingerie shop.

"No. But I thought of it because I saw them. I go to Fisher's for my brassieres."

"Boulevard Montparnasse?" Rirette cried. "Look out, Lulu," she went on gravely, "better not hang around the Boulevard Montparnasse, especially now: we'd run into Henri and that would be most unpleasant."

"Henri?" said Lulu, shrugging her shoulders; "Of course not. Why?"

Indignation flushed purple on Rirette's cheeks and temples.

"You're still the same, Lulu, when you don't like something, you deny it, pure and simple. You want to go to Fisher's so you insist Henri won't be on the Boulevard Montparnasse. You know very well he goes by every day at six, it's his way home. You told me that yourself: he goes up the Rue de Rennes and waits for the bus at the corner of the Boulevard Raspail."

"First, it's only five o'clock," Lulu said, "and besides, maybe he didn't go to the office: the note I wrote must have knocked him out."

"But, Lulu," Rirette said suddenly, "You know there's another Fisher's not far from the Opera, on the Rue du Quartre Septembre."

"Yes," Lulu said weakly, "but it's so far to go there."

"Well, I like that; so far to go. It's only two minutes from here. it's a lot closer than Montparnasse."

"I don't like their things."

Rirette thought with amusement that all the Fishers sold the same things.

But Lulu was incomprehensibly obstinate: Henri was positively the last person on earth she would want to meet now and you'd think she was purposely throwing herself in his way.

"Well," she said indulgently, "if we meet him, we meet him, that's all. He isn't going to eat us."

Lulu insisted on going to Montparnasse on foot; she said she needed air. They followed the Rue de Seine, then the Rue de L'Odéon and the Rue de Vaugirard. Rirette praised Pierre and showed Lulu how perfect he had been under the circumstances.

"How I love Paris," Lulu said, "I'm going to miss it!"

"Oh be quiet, Lulu, when I think how lucky you are to go to Nice and then you say how much you'll miss Paris."

Lulu did not answer, she began looking right and left sadly, searching.

When they came out of Fisher's they heard six o'clock strike. Rirette took Lulu's elbow and tried to hurry her along, but Lulu stopped before Baumann the florist.

"Look at those azaleas, Rirette. If I had a nice living room I'd have them everywhere."

"I don't like potted plants," Rirette said.

She was exasperated. She turned her head toward the Rue

de Rennes and sure enough, after a minute, she saw Henri's great stupid silhouette appear. He was bare-headed, and wearing a brown tweed sport coat. Rirette hated brown: "There he is, Lulu, there he is," she said hurriedly.

"Where?" Lulu asked. "Where is he?"

She was scarcely more calm than Rirette.

"Behind us, on the other side of the street. Run and don't turn around."

Lulu turned around anyhow.

"I see him," she said.

Rirette tried to drag her away, but Lulu stiffened and stared at Henri. At last she said, "I think he saw us."

She seemed frightened, suddenly yielded to Rirette and let herself be taken away quietly.

"Now for Heaven's sake, Lulu, don't turn around again," Rirette said breathlessly. "We'll turn down the first street on the right, Rue Delambre."

They walked very quickly, jostling the passers-by. At times Lulu held back a little, or sometimes it was she who dragged Rirette. But they had not quite reached the corner of the Rue Delambre when Rirette saw a large brown shadow behind Lulu; she knew it was Henri and began shaking with anger. Lulu kept her eyes lowered, she looked sly and determined. She's regretting her mistake, but it's too late. Too bad for her.

They hurried on; Henri followed them without a word. They passed the Rue Delambre and kept walking in the direction of the Observatoire. Rirette heard the squeak of Henri's shoes; there was also a sort of light, regular rattle that kept time with their steps: it was his breathing (Henri always breathed heavily, but never that much; he must have run to catch up with them or else it was emotion).

We must act as if he weren't there, Rirette thought. Pretend not to notice his existence. But she could not keep from looking out of the corner of her eye. He was white as a sheet and his eyelids were so lowered they seemed shut. Almost looks like a sleepwalker, thought Rirette with a sort of horror. Henri's lips were trembling and a little bit of pink gauze trembled on the lower lip. And the breathing—that hoarse, even breathing, now ending with a sort of nasal music. Rirette felt uncomfortable: she was not afraid of Henri, but sickness and passion always frightened her a little. After a moment, Henri put his hand out gently and took Lulu's arm. Lulu twisted her mouth as if she were going to cry and pulled it away, shuddering.

Henri went "Phew!"

Rirette had a mad desire to stop: she had a stitch in the side and her ears were ringing. But Lulu was almost running; she too looked like a sleepwalker. Rirette had the feeling that if she let go of Lulu's arm and stopped, they would both keep on running side by side, mute, pale as death, their eyes closed.

Henri began to speak. With a strange, hoarse voice he said: "Come back with me."

Lulu did not answer. Henri said again, in the same toneless voice:

"You are my wife. Come back with me."

"You can see she doesn't want to go back," Rirette answered between her teeth. "Leave her alone."

He did not seem to hear her. "I am your husband," he repeated. "I want you to come back with me."

"For God's sake let her alone," Rirette said sharply. "Bothering her like that won't do any good, so shut up and let her be."

"She is my wife," he said, "she belongs to me, I want her to come back with me."

He had taken Lulu's arm and this time Lulu did not shake him off.

"Go away," Rirette said.

"I won't go away, I'll follow her everywhere, I want her to come back home."

He spoke with effort. Suddenly he made a grimace which showed his teeth and shouted with all his might:

"You belong to me!"

Some people turned around, laughing. Henri shook Lulu's arm, curled back his lips and howled like an animal. Luckily an empty taxi passed. Rirette waved at it and the taxi stopped. Henri stopped too. Lulu wanted to keep on walking but they held her firmly, each by one arm.

"You ought to know," said Rirette, pulling Lulu towards the street, "You'll never get her back with violence."

"Let her alone, let my wife alone," Henri said, pulling in the opposite direction. Lulu was limp as a bag of laundry.

"Are you getting in or not?" the taxi driver called impatiently.

Rirette dropped Lulu's arm and rained blows on Henri's hand. But he did not seem to feel them. After a moment he let go and began to look at Rirette stupidly. Rirette looked at him too. She could barely collect her thoughts, an immense sickness filled her. They stayed, eye to eye, for a few seconds, both breathing heavily. Then Rirette pulled herself together, took Lulu by the waist and drew her to the taxi.

"Where to?" the driver asked.

Henri had followed. He wanted to get in with them. But Rirette pushed him back with all her strength and closed the door quickly.

"Drive, drive!" she told the chauffeur. "We'll tell you the address later."

The taxi started up and Rirette dropped to the back of the car. How vulgar it all was, she thought. She hated Lulu.

Where do you want to go, Lulu?" she asked sweetly.

Lulu did not answer. Rirette put her arms around her and became persuasive.

"You must answer me. Do you want me to drop you off at Pierre's?"

Lulu made a movement Rirette took for acquiescence. She leaned forward: "11 Rue Messine."

When Rirette turned around again, Lulu was watching her strangely.

"What the . . . ," Rirette began.

"I hate you," Lulu screamed, "I hate Pierre, I hate Henri. What do you all have against me? You're torturing me."

She stopped short and her features clouded.

"Cry," Rirette said with calm dignity, "cry, it'll do you good."

Lulu bent double and began to sob. Rirette took her in her arms and held her close. From time to time she stroked her hair. But inside she felt cold and distrustful. Lulu was calm when the cab stopped. She wiped her eyes and powdered her nose.

"Excuse me," she said gently, "it was nerves. I couldn't bear seeing him like that, it hurt me."

"He looked like an orangoutang," said Rirette, once more serene.

Lulu smiled.

"When will I see you again?" Rirette asked.

"Oh, not before tomorrow. You know Pierre can't put me up because of his mother. I'll be at the Hotel du Théatre. You could come early, around nine, if it doesn't put you out, because after that I'm going to see Mama."

She was pale and Rirette thought sadly of the terrible ease with which she could break down.

"Don't worry too much tonight," she said.

"I'm awfully tired," Lulu said, "I hope Pierre will let me go back early, but he never understands those things."

Rirette kept the taxi and was driven home. For a moment she thought she'd go to the movies, but she had no heart for it. She threw her hat on a chair and took a step towards the window. But the bed attracted her, all white, all soft and moist in its shadowy hollows. To throw herself on it, to feel the caress of the pillow against her burning cheeks. I'm strong. I did everything for Lulu and now I'm all alone and no one does anything for me. She had so much pity for herself that she felt a flood of sobs mounting in her throat. They're going to go to Nice and I won't see them any more. I'm the one who made them happy but they won't think about me. And I'll stay here working eight hours a day selling artificial pearls in Burma's. When the first tears rolled down her cheeks she let herself fall softly on the bed. "Nice," she repeated, weeping bitterly, "Nice . . . in the sunlight . . . on the Riviera. . . ."

IV

"Phew!"

Black night. You'd think somebody was walking around the room: a man in slippers. He put one foot out cautiously, then the other, unable to avoid a light cracking of the floor. He stopped, there was a moment of silence, then, suddenly transported to the other end of the room, he began his aimless, idiotic walking again. Lulu was cold, the blankets were much too light. She said *Phew* aloud and the sound of her voice frightened her.

Phew! I'm sure he's looking at the sky and the stars now, he's lighting a cigarette, he's outside, he said he liked the purple color of the Paris sky. With little steps, he goes back, with little steps: he feels poetic just after he's done it, he told me, and light as a cow that's just been milked, he doesn't think any more about it—and me, I'm defiled. It doesn't surprise me that he's pure now that he left his own dirt here, in the blackness, there's a hand towel full of it and the sheet's wet in the middle of the bed, I can't stretch out my legs because I'll feel the wet on my skin, what filth and him all dry, I heard him whistle under my window when he left; he was down there dry and fresh in his fine clothes and topcoat, you must admit he knows how to dress, a woman would be proud to go out with him, he was under the window and I was naked in the blackness and I was cold and rubbed my belly with my hands because I thought I was still wet. I'll come up for a minute, he said, just to see your room. He stayed two hours and the bed creaked—this rotten little iron bed. I wonder where he found out about this hotel, he told me he spent two weeks here once, that I'd be all right here, these are funny rooms, I saw two of them, I never saw such little rooms cluttered up with furniture, cushions and couches and little tables, it stinks of love, I don't know whether he stayed here two weeks but he surely didn't stay alone; he can't have much respect for me to stick me in here. The bellboy laughed when we went up, an Algerian, I hate those people, he looked at my legs, then he went into the office, he must have thought, That's it, they're going to do it, and imagined all sorts of dirty things, they say it's terrible what they do with women down there; if they ever get hold of one she limps for the rest of her life; and all the time Pierre was bothering me I was thinking about that Algerian who was thinking about what I was doing and thinking a lot of dirtiness worse than it was. Somebody's in this room!

Lulu held her breath but the creaking stopped immediately. I have a pain between my thighs, it itches, I want to cry and it will be like that every night except tomorrow night because we'll be on the train. Lulu bit her lip and shuddered because she remembered she had groaned. It's not true, I didn't groan, I simply breathed hard a little because he's so heavy, when he's on me he takes my breath away. He said, "You're groaning, you're coming." I hate people to talk to me when I'm doing that, I wish they'd forget but he never stops saying a lot of dirty things. I didn't groan, in the first place, I can't have any pleasure, it's a fact, the doctor said so, unless I do it to myself. He won't believe it, they never want to believe it, they all said: "It's because you got off to a bad start, I'll teach you"; I let them talk, I knew what the trouble was, it's medical; but that provokes them.

Someone was coming up the stairs. Someone coming back. God, don't let him come back. He's capable of doing it if he feels like it again. It isn't him, those are heavy steps—or else—Lulu's heart jumped in her breast—if it was the Algerian, he knows I'm alone, he's going to knock on the door, I can't, I can't stand that, no, it's the floor below, it's a man going in, he's putting his key in the lock, he's taking his time, he's drunk, I wonder who lives in this hotel, it must be a fine bunch; I met a redhead this afternoon, on the stairs, she had eyes like a dope fiend. I didn't groan.

Of course, he did manage to bother me with all his feeling around, he knows how; I have a horror of men who know how, I'd rather sleep with a virgin. Those hands going right to where they want, pressing a little, not too much . . . they take you for an instrument they're proud of knowing how to play. I hate people to bother me, my throat's dry, I'm afraid and I have a bad taste in my mouth and I'm humiliated because they think he dominates me, I'd like to slap Pierre when he put on his elegant airs and says, "I've got technique." My God, to think that's life, that's why you get dressed and wash and make yourself pretty and all the books are written about that and you think about it all the time and finally that's what it is, you go to a room with somebody who half smothers you and ends up by wetting your stomach. I want to sleep. Oh, if I could only sleep a little bit, tomorrow I'll travel all night, I'll be all in. Still I'd like to be a little fresh to walk around Nice; they say it's so lovely, little Italian streets and colored clothes drying in the sun, I'll set myself up with my easel and I'll paint and the little girls will come to see what I'm doing. Rot! (She had stretched out a little and her hip touched the damp spot in the sheet.) That's all he brought me here for. Nobody, nobody loves me. He walked beside me and I almost fainted and I waited for one tender word, he could have said, "I love you." I wouldn't have gone back to him, of course, but I'd have said something nice, we would have parted good friends, I waited and waited, he took my arm and I let him, Rirette was furious, it's not true he looked like an orangoutang but I knew she was thinking something like that, she was watching him out of the corner of her eye, nastily, it's amazing how nasty she can be, well, in spite of that, when he took my arm I didn't resist but it wasn't *me* he wanted, he wanted his wife because he married me and he's my husband; he always depreciated me, he said he was more intelligent than I and everything that happened is all his fault, he didn't need to treat me so high and mighty, I'd still be with him. I'm sure he doesn't miss me now, he isn't crying, he's raving, that's what he's doing and he's glad to have the bed all to himself so he can stretch his long legs out. I'd like to die. I'm so afraid he'll think badly of me; I couldn't explain anything to him because Rirette was between us, talking, talking, she looked hysterical. Now she's glad, she's complimenting herself on her courage, how rotten that is with Henri who's gentle as a lamb. I'll go. They can't make me leave him like a dog. She jumped out of bed and turned the switch. My stockings and slip are enough. She was in such a hurry that she did not even take the trouble to comb her hair. And the people who see me won't know I'm naked under my heavy grey coat, it comes down to my feet. The Algerian—she stopped, her heart pounding—I'll have to wake him up to open the door. She went down on tiptoe—but the steps creaked one by one; she knocked at the office window.

"Who is it?" the Algerian asked. His eyes were red and his hair tousled, he didn't look very frightening.

"Open the door for me," Lulu said dryly.

Fifteen minutes later she rang at Henri's door.

V

"Who's there?" Henri asked through the door.

"It's me."

He doesn't answer, he doesn't want to let me in my own home. But I'll knock on the door till he opens, he'll give in because of the neighbors. After a minute the door was half opened and Henri appeared, pale, with a pimple on his nose; he was in pajamas. He hasn't slept, Lulu thought tenderly.

"I didn't want to leave like that, I wanted to see you again."

Henri still said nothing. Lulu entered, pushing him aside a little. How stupid he is, he's always in your way, he's looking at me with round eyes with his arms hanging, he doesn't know what to do with his body. Shut up, shut up, I see you're moved and you can't speak. He made an effort to swallow his saliva and Lulu had to close the door.

"I want us to part good friends," she said.

He opened his mouth as if to speak, turned suddenly and fled. What's he doing? She dared not follow him. Is he crying? Suddenly she heard him cough: he's in the bathroom. When he came back she hung about his neck and pressed her mouth against his: he smelled of vomit. Lulu burst out sobbing.

"I'm cold," Henri said.

"Let's go to bed," she said, weeping. "I can stay till tomorrow morning."

They went to bed and Lulu was shaken with enormous sobs because she found her room and bed clean and the red glow in the window. She thought Henri would take her in his arms but he did nothing: he was sleeping stretched out full length as if someone had put a poker in the bed. He's as stiff as when he talks to a Swiss. She took his head in her two hands and stared at him. "You are pure, pure." He began to cry.

"I'm miserable," he said, "I've never been so miserable."

"I haven't either," Lulu said.

They wept for a long time. After a while she put out the light and laid her head on his shoulder. If we could stay like that forever: pure and sad as two orphans; but it isn't possible, it doesn't happen in life. Life was an enormous wave breaking on Lulu, tearing her from the arms of Henri. Your hand, your big hand. He's proud of them because they're big, he says that descendants of old families always have big limbs. He won't take my waist in his hand any more. He tickled me a little but I was proud because he could almost make his fingers meet. It isn't true that he's impotent—he's pure, pure and a little lazy. She smiled through her tears and kissed him under the chin.

"What am I going to tell my parents?" Henri asked. "My mother'll die when she hears."

Mme. Crispin would not die, on the contrary, she would triumph. They'll talk about me, at meals, all five of them, blaming me, like people who know a lot about things but don't want to say everything because of the kid who's sixteen and she's too young to talk about certain things in front of her. She'll laugh inside herself because she knows it all, she always knows it all and she detests me. All this muck. And appearances are against me.

"Don't tell them right away," she pleaded, "tell them I'm at Nice for my health."

"They won't believe me."

She kissed Henri quickly all over his face.

"Henri, you weren't nice enough to me."

"That's true," Henri said, "I wasn't nice enough. Neither were you," he reflected, "you weren't nice enough."

"I wasn't. Ah!" Lulu said, "how miserable we are!" She cried so loudly she thought she would suffocate: soon it would be day and she would leave. You never, never do what you want, you're carried away.

"You shouldn't have left like that," said Henri.

Lulu sighed. "I loved you a lot, Henri."

"And now you don't?"

"It isn't the same."

"Who are you leaving with?"

"People you don't know."

"How do you know people I don't know?" Henri asked angrily, "Where did you meet them?"

"Never mind, darling, my little Gulliver, you aren't going to act like a husband now?"

"You're leaving with a man," Henri said, weeping.

"Listen, Henri, I swear I'm not, I swear, men disgust me now. I'm leaving with a family, with friends of Rirette, old people. I want to live alone, they'll find a job for me; Oh Henri, if you knew how much I needed to live alone, how it all disgusts me."

"What?" Henri asked, "what disgusts you?"

"Everything!" She kissed him. "You're the only one that doesn't disgust me, darling."

She passed her hands under Henri's pajamas and caressed his whole body. He shuddered under her icy hands but he did not turn away, he said only, "I'm going to get sick."

Surely, something was broken in him.

At seven o'clock, Lulu got up, her eyes swollen with tears. She said wearily, "I have to go back there."

"Back where?"

"Hotel du Théâtre, Rue Vandamme. A rotten hotel."

"Stay with me."

"No, Henri, please, don't insist. I told you it was impossible."

The flood carries you away; that's life; we can't judge or understand, we can only let ourselves drift. Tomorrow I'll be in Nice. She went to the bathroom to wash her eyes with warm water. She put on her coat, shivering. It's like fate. I only hope I can sleep on the train tonight, or else I'll be completely knocked out when I get to Nice. I hope he got first-class tickets; that'll be the first time I ever rode first class. Everything is always like that: for years I've wanted to take a long trip first class, and the day it happens it works out so that I can't enjoy it. She was in a hurry to leave now, for these last moments had been unbearable.

"What are you going to do with that Gallois person?" she asked.

Gallois had ordered a poster from Henri, Henri had made it and now Gallois didn't want it any more.

"I don't know," Henri said.

He was crouched under the covers, only his hair and the end of his ear was visible. Slowly and softly, he said, "I'd like to sleep for a week."

"Goodbye, darling," Lulu said.

"Goodbye."

She bent over him, drawing aside the covers a little, and kissed him on the forehead. She stayed a long while on the landing without deciding to close the door of the apartment. After a moment, she turned her eyes away and pulled the knob violently. She heard a dry noise and thought she was going to faint: she had felt like that when they threw the first shovelful of earth on her father's casket.

Henri hasn't been nice. He could have gotten up and gone as far as the door with me. I think I would have minded less if he had been the one who closed it.

VI

"She did that!" said Rirette, with a far-off look. "She did that!"

It was evening. About six Pierre had called Rirette and she had met him at the *Dôme*.

"But you," Pierre said, "weren't you supposed to see her this morning at nine?"

"I saw her."

"She didn't look strange?"

"No indeed," Rirette said, "I didn't notice anything. She was a little tired but she told me she hadn't slept after you left because she was so excited about seeing Nice and she was a little afraid of the Algerian bellboy. . . . Wait . . . she even asked me if I thought you'd bought first-class tickets on the train, she said it was the dream of her life to travel first class. No," Rirette decided, "I'm sure she didn't have anything like that in mind; at least not while I was there. I stayed with her for two hours and I can tell those things, I'd be surprised if I missed anything. You tell me she's very close-mouthed but I've known her for four years and I've seen her in all sort of situations. I know Lulu through and through."

"Then the Texiers made her mind up. It's funny. . . ." He mused a few moments and suddenly began again. "I wonder who gave them Lulu's address. I picked out the hotel and she'd never heard of it before."

He toyed distractedly with Lulu's letter and Rirette was annoyed because she wanted to read it and he hadn't offered it to her.

"When did you get it?" she asked, finally.

"The letter? . . ." He handed it to her with simplicity. "Here, you can read it. She must have given it to the concierge around one o'clock."

It was a thin, violet sheet such as is sold in cigar stores:

Dearest Darling.

The Texiers came (I don't know who gave them the address) and I'm going to cause you a lot of sorrow, but I'm not going, dearest, darling Pierre; I am staying with Henri because he is too unhappy. They went to see him this morning, he didn't want to open the door and Mme. Texier said he didn't look human. They were very nice and they understood my reasons, they said all the wrong was on his side, that he was a bear but at heart he wasn't bad. She said he needed that to make him understand how much he needed me. I don't know who gave them the address, they didn't say, they must have happened to see me when I was leaving the hotel this morning with Rirette. Mme. Texier said she knew she was asking me to make an enormous sacrifice but that she knew me well enough to know that I wouldn't sneak out. I'll miss our lovely trip to Nice very much, darling, but I thought you would be less unhappy because I am still yours. I am yours with all my heart and all my body and we shall see each other as often as before. But Henri would kill himself if he didn't have me any more. I am indispensable to him; I assure you that it doesn't amuse me to feel such a responsibility. I hope you won't make your naughty little face which frightens me so, you wouldn't want me to be sorry, would you? I am going back to Henri soon, I'm a little sick when I think that I'm going to see him in such a state but I will have the courage to name my own conditions. First, I want more freedom because I love you and I want him to leave Robert alone and not say anything bad about Mama any more, ever. Dearest, I am so sad, I wish you could be here, I want you, I press myself against you and I feel your caresses in all my body. I will be at the Dôme tomorrow at five.

LULU

"Poor Pierre."
Rirette took his hand.

"I'll tell you," Pierre said, "I feel sorry for her. She needed air and sunshine. But since she decided that way. . . . My mother made a frightful scene," he went on. "The villa belongs to her, she didn't want me to take a woman there."

"Ah?" Rirette said, in a broken voice, "Ah? So everything's all right, then, everybody's happy!"

She dropped Pierre's hand: without knowing why she felt flooded with bitter regret.

THE CHILDHOOD
OF A LEADER

"I look adorable in my little angel's costume." Mme. Portier told
mamma: "Your little boy looks good enough to eat. He's simply
adorable in his little angel's costume." M. Bouffardier drew Lucien between his knees and stroked his arm: "A real little girl,"
he said, smiling. "What's your name? Jacqueline, Lucienne,
Margot?" Lucien turned red and said, "My name is Lucien." He
was no longer quite sure about not being a little girl: a lot of
people had kissed him and called him mademoiselle, everybody
thought he was so charming with his gauze wings, his long blue
robe, small bare arms and blond curls: he was afraid that the
people would suddenly decide he wasn't a little boy any more;
he would have protested in vain, no one would listen to him, they
wouldn't let him take off his dress any more except to sleep and
every morning when he woke up he would find it at the foot of
his bed and when he wanted to wee-wee during the day, he'd
have to lift it up like Nenette and sit on his heels. Everybody
would say: my sweet little darling; maybe it's happened already
and I *am* a little girl; he felt so soft inside that it made him a
little sick and his voice came out of his mouth like a flute and he
offered flowers to everybody in rounded, curved gestures; he
wanted to kiss his soft upper arm. He thought: it isn't real. He
liked things that weren't real, but he had a better time on Mardi
Gras: they dressed him up as Pierrot, he ran and jumped and
shouted with Riri and they hid under the tables. His mother gave
him a light tap with her lorgnette. "I'm proud of my little boy."
She was impressive and beautiful, the fattest and biggest of all
these ladies. When he passed in front of the long buffet covered
with a white tablecloth, his papa who was drinking a glass of
champagne, lifted him up and said, "Little man!" Lucien felt like
crying and saying, "Nah!" He asked for orangeade because it was
cold and they had forbidden him to drink it. But they poured

84

him some in a tiny glass. It had a pithy taste and wasn't as cold as they said: Lucien began to think about the orangeade with castor oil he swallowed when he was sick. He burst out sobbing and found it comforting to sit between papa and mama in the car. Mama pressed Lucien against her, she was hot and perfumed and all in silk. From time to time the inside of the car grew white as chalk, Lucien blinked his eyes, the violets mama was wearing on her corsage came out of the shadows and Lucien suddenly smelled their perfume. He was still sobbing a little but he felt moist and itchy, somewhat pithy like the orangeade; he would have liked to splash in his little bathtub and have mama wash him with the rubber sponge. They let him sleep in papa and mama's room because he was a little baby; he laughed and made the springs of his little bed jingle and papa said, "The child is over-excited." He drank a little orange-blossom water and saw papa in shirtsleeves.

The next day Lucien was sure he had forgotten something. He remembered the dream he had very clearly: papa and mama were wearing angels' robes, Lucien was sitting all naked on his pot beating a drum, papa and mama flew around him; it was a nightmare. But there had been something before the dream, Lucien must have wakened. When he tried to remember, he saw a long black tunnel lit by a small blue lamp like the night-light they turned on in his parents' room every evening. At the very bottom of this dark blue night something went past—something white. He sat on the ground at mama's feet and took his drum. Mama asked him, "Why are you looking at me like that, darling?" He lowered his eyes and beat on his drum, crying, "Boom, boom, taraboom." But when she turned her head he began to scrutinize her minutely as if he were seeing her for the first time. He recognized the blue robe with the pink stuff and the face too. Yet it wasn't the same. Suddenly he thought he had it; if he thought about it a tiny bit more, he would find what he was looking for. The tunnel lit up with a pale grey light and he could see something moving. Lucien was afraid and cried out. The tunnel disappeared. "What's the matter, little darling?" Mama asked. She was kneeling close to him and looked worried. "I'm having fun," Lucien said. Mama smelled good but he was afraid she would touch him: she looked funny to him, papa too. He decided he would never sleep in their room any more.

Mama noticed nothing the following day. Lucien was always under her feet, as usual, and he gossiped with her like a real little man. He asked her to tell him Little Red Riding-hood and mama took him on her knees. She talked about the wolf and Little Red Riding-hood's grandmother, with finger raised, smiling and grave, Lucien looked at her and said, "And then what?" And sometimes he touched the little hairs on the back of her neck; but he wasn't listening, he was wondering if she were his real mother. When she finished, he said, "Mama, tell me about when you were a little girl." And mama told him; but maybe she was lying. Maybe she was a little boy before and they put dresses on her—like Lucien, the other night—and she kept on wearing them to act like a little girl. Gently he felt her beautiful fat arms which were soft as butter under the silk. What would happen if they took off mama's dress and she put on papa's pants? Maybe right away she'd grow a black moustache. He clasped mama's arms with all his might; he had a feeling she was going to be transformed into a horrible beast before his eyes—or maybe turn into a bearded lady like the one in the carnival. She laughed, opening her mouth wide, and Lucien saw her pink tongue and the back of her throat: it was dirty, he wanted to spit in it. "Hahaha!" Mama said, "how you hug me, little man. Hug me tight. As tight as you love me." Lucien took one of her lovely hands with the silver rings on it and covered it with kisses. But the next day when she was sitting near him holding his hands while he was on the pot and said to him, "Push, Lucien, push, little darling . . . please." He suddenly stopped pushing and asked her, a little breathlessly, "But you're my real mother, aren't you?" She said, "Silly," and asked him if it wasn't going to come soon. From the day Lucien was sure she was playing a joke on him and he never again told her he would marry her when he grew up. But he was not quite sure what the joke was: maybe one night in the tunnel, robbers came and took papa and mama and put those two in their place. Or maybe it was really papa and mama but during the day they played one part and at night they were all different. Lucien was hardly surprised on Christmas Eve when he suddenly woke up and saw them putting toys in front of the fireplace. The next day they talked about Père Noël and Lucien pretended he believed them: he thought it was their role, they must have stolen the toys. He had scarlatina in February and had a lot of fun.

After he was cured, he got in the habit of playing orphan. He sat under the chestnut tree in the middle of the lawn, filling his hands with earth, and thought: I'm an orphan. I'm going to call myself Louis. I haven't eaten for six days. Germaine, the maid, called him to lunch and at table he kept on playing; papa and mama noticed nothing. He had been picked up by robbers who wanted to make a pickpocket out of him. After he had eaten he would run away and denounce them. He ate and drank very little; he had read in *L'Auberge de l'Ange Gardien* that the first meal of a starving man should be light. It was amusing because everybody was playing. Papa and mama were playing papa and mama; mama was playing worried because her little darling wasn't eating, papa was playing at reading the paper and sometimes shaking his finger in Lucien's face saying, "Badaboom, little man!" And Lucien was playing too, but finally he didn't know at what. Orphan? Or Lucien? He looked at the water bottle. There was a little red light dancing in the bottom of the water and he would have sworn papa's hand was in the water bottle, enormous, luminous, with little black hairs on the fingers. Lucien suddenly felt that the water bottle was playing at being a water bottle. He barely touched his food and he was so hungry in the afternoon that he stole a dozen plums and almost had indigestion. He thought he had enough of playing Lucien.

Still, he could not stop himself and it seemed to him that he was always playing. He wanted to be like M. Bouffardier who was so ugly and serious. When M. Bouffardier came to dinner, he bent over mama's hand and said, "Your servant, dear madame," and Lucien planted himself in the middle of the salon and watched him with admiration. But nothing serious happened to Lucien. When he fell down and bumped himself, he sometimes stopped crying and wondered, "Do I really hurt?" Then he felt even sadder and his tears flowed more than ever. When he kissed mama's hand and said, "Your servant, dear madame," she rumpled his hair and said, "It isn't nice, little mouse, you mustn't make fun of grown-ups," and felt all discouraged. The only important things he could find were the first and third Fridays of the month. Those days a lot of ladies came to see mama and two or three were always in mourning; Lucien loved ladies in mourning especially when they had big feet. Generally, he liked grown-ups because they were so respectable—and you could never imagine they forgot themselves in bed or did all the other things little boys do, because they have so many dark clothes on their bodies and you can't imagine what's underneath. When they're all together they eat everything and talk and even their laughs are serious, it's beautiful, like at mass. They treated Lucien like a grown-up person. Mme. Couffin took Lucien on her lap and felt his calves, declaring, "He's the prettiest, cutest one I've seen." Then she questioned him about his likes and dislikes, kissed him and asked him what he would do when he was big. And sometimes he answered he'd be a great general like Joan of Arc and he'd take back Alsace-Lorraine from the Germans, or sometimes he wanted to be a missionary. As he spoke, he believed what he said. Mme. Besse was a large, strong woman with a slight moustache. She romped with Lucien, tickled him and called him "my little doll." Lucien was overjoyed, he laughed easily and squirmed under the ticklings; he thought he was a little doll, a charming little doll for the grown-ups and he would have liked Mme. Besse to undress him and wash him like a rubber doll and send him bye-bye in a tiny little cradle. And sometimes Mme. Besse asked, "And does my little doll talk?" and she squeezed his stomach suddenly. Then Lucien pretended to be a mechanical doll and said, "Crick!" in a muffled voice and they both laughed.

The curé who came to the house every Saturday asked him if he loved his mother. Lucien adored his pretty mama and his papa who was so strong and good. He answered, "Yes," looking the curé straight in the eyes with a little air of boldness that made everybody laugh. The curé had a face like a raspberry, red and lumpy with a hair on each lump. He told Lucien it was very nice and that he should always love his mama; then he asked who Lucien preferred, his mother or God. Lucien could not guess the answer on the spot and he began to shake his curls and stamp his feet shouting, "Baroom, tarataraboom!" and the grown-ups continued their conversation as though he did not exist. He ran to the garden and slipped out by the back door; he had brought his little reed cane with him. Naturally, Lucien was never supposed to leave the garden, it was forbidden; usually Lucien was a good little boy but that day he felt like disobeying. He looked defiantly at the big nettle patch; you could see it was a forbidden place; the wall was black, the nettles were naughty, harmful plants, a dog had done his business just at the foot of the nettles; it smelled of plants, dog dirt and hot wine. Lucien lashed at the nettles with his cane crying "I love my mama, I love my mama." He saw the broken nettles hanging sadly, oozing a white juice, their whitish, down necks had unravelled in breaking, he heard a small solitary voice which cried, "I love my mama, I love my mama"; a big blue fly was buzzing around: a horsefly, Lucien was afraid of it—and a forbidden, powerful odor, putrid and peaceful, filled his nostrils. He repeated, "I love my mama," but his voice seemed strange, he felt deep terror and ran back into the salon, like a flash. From that day on, Lucien understood that he did not love his mama. He did not feel guilty but redoubled his niceties because he thought he should pretend to love his parents all his life, or else he was a naughty little boy. Mme. Fleurier found Lucien more and more tender and just then there was the war and papa went off to fight and mama was glad, in her sorrow, that Lucien was so full of attention; in the afternoons, when she rested on her beach chair in the garden because she was so full of sorrow, he ran to get her a cushion and slipped it beneath her head or put a blanket over her legs and she protested, laughing, "But I'll be too hot, my little man, how sweet you are!" He kissed her furiously, all out of breath, saying, "My own mama," and sat down at the foot of the chestnut tree.

He said, "chestnut tree," and waited. But nothing happened. Mama was stretched out on the verandah, all tiny at the bottom of a heavy stifling silence. There was a smell of hot grass, you could play explorer in the jungle; but Lucien did not feel like playing. The air trembled about the red crest of the wall and the sunlight made burning spots on the earth and on Lucien's hands. "Chestnut tree!" It was shocking: when Lucien told mama, "My pretty little mama" she smiled and when he called Germaine "stinkweed" she cried and went complaining to mama. But when he said "chestnut tree," nothing at all happened. He muttered between his teeth, "Nasty old tree," and was not reassured, but since the tree did not move he repeated, louder, "Nasty old tree, nasty old chestnut tree, you wait, you just wait and see!" and he kicked it. But the tree stayed still—just as though it were made of wood. That evening at dinner Lucien told mama, "You know, mama, the trees, well . . . they're made out of wood," making a surprised little face which mama liked. But Mme. Fleurier had received no mail at noon. She said dryly, "Don't act like a fool." Lucien became a little roughneck. He broke his toys to see how they were made, he whittled the arm of a chair with one of papa's old razors, he knocked down a tanagra figure in the living room to see if it were hollow and if there were anything inside; when he walked he struck the heads from plants and flowers with his cane: each time he was deeply disappointed, things were stupid, nothing really and truly existed. Often mama showed him flowers and asked him, "What's the name of this?" But Lucien shook his head and answered, "That isn't anything, that doesn't have any name." All that wasn't worth bothering with. It was much more fun to pull the legs off a grasshopper because they throbbed between your fingers like a top and a yellow cream came out when you pressed its stomach. But even so, the grasshoppers didn't make any noise. Lucien would have liked to torture an animal that cried when it was hurt, a chicken for instance, but he didn't dare go near them. M. Fleurier came back in March because he was a manager and the general told him he would be much more useful at the head of his factory than in the trenches like just anybody. He thought Lucien had changed very much and said he didn't recognize his little man any more. Lucien had fallen into a sort of somnolence; he answered quickly, he always had a finger in his nose or else he breathed on his fingers and smelled them and he had to be begged to do his little business. Now he went alone to the bathroom; he had only to leave the door half open and from time to time, mama or Germaine came to encourage him. He stayed whole hours on the throne and once he was so bored he went to sleep. The doctor said he was growing too quickly and prescribed a tonic. Mama wanted to teach Lucien new games but Lucien thought he played enough as it was and anyhow all games were the same, it was always the same thing. He often pouted: it was also a game and rather amusing. It hurt mama, you felt all sad and resentful, you got a little deaf and your mouth was pursed up and your eyes misty, inside it was warm and soft like when you're under the sheets at night and smell your own odor; you were alone in the world. Lucien could no longer leave his broodings and when papa put on his mocking voice to tell him, "You're going to hatch chickens," Lucien rolled on the ground and sobbed. He still went to the salon when mama was having visitors, but since they had cut off his curls the grown-ups paid less attention to him unless it was to point out a moral for him and tell him instructive stories. When his cousin Riri and Aunt Bertha, his pretty mama, came to Ferolles because of the bombings, Lucien was very glad and tried to teach him how to play. But Riri was too busy hating the Boches and he still smelled like a baby even though he was six months older than Lucien; he had freckles and didn't always understand things very well. However, Lucien confided to him that he walked in his sleep. Some people get up at night and talk and walk around still sleeping: Lucien had read that in the *Petit Explorateur* and he thought there must be a real Lucien who talked, walked, and really loved his parents at night, only as soon as morning came, he forgot everything and began to pretend to be Lucien. In the beginning Lucien only half believed this story but one day they went near the nettles and Riri showed Lucien his wee-wee and told him, "Look how big it is, I'm a big boy. When it'll be all big I'll be a man and I'll go and fight the Boches in the trenches." Lucien thought Riri was funny and he burst out laughing. "Let's see yours," Riri said. They compared and Lucien's was smaller but Riri cheated: he pulled his to make it longer. "I have the biggest," Riri said. "Yes, but I'm a sleepwalker," Lucien said calmly. Riri didn't know what a sleepwalker was and Lucien had to explain it to him. When he finished, he thought, "Then it's true I'm a sleepwalker," and he had a terrible desire to cry. Since they slept in the same bed they agreed that Riri would stay up the next night and watch Lucien when Lucien got up and remember all he said. "You wake me up after a while," Lucien said, "to see if I remember anything I did." That night, Lucien, unable to sleep, heard sharp snores and had to wake up Riri. "Zanzibar!" Riri said. "Wake up, Riri, you have to watch me when I get up." "Let me sleep," Riri said in a thick, pasty voice. Lucien shook him and pinched him under his shirt and Riri began to jump around and he stayed awake, his eyes open and a funny smile on his lips. Lucien thought about a bicycle his father was to buy him, he heard a train whistle and suddenly the maid came in and opened the curtains, it was eight o'clock in the morning. Lucien never knew what he did during the night. But God knew because God knew everything. Lucien knelt on the prie-dieu and forced himself to behave so that his mama would congratulate him after mass but he hated God: God knew more about Lucien than Lucien himself. God knew that Lucien didn't love his mama or papa and that he pretended to be good and touched his wee-wee in bed at night. Luckily, God couldn't remember everything because there were so many little boys in the world. When Lucien tapped his forehead and said, "Picotin," right away God forgot everything he had seen. Lucien also undertook to persuade God that he loved his mama. From time to time he said in his head, "How I love my dear mama!" There was always a little corner in him which wasn't quite persuaded and of course God saw that corner. In that case, He won. But sometimes you could absorb yourself so completely in what you were saying. You said very quickly, "Oh how I love my mama," pronouncing it carefully and you saw mama's face and felt all tender, you thought vaguely, vaguely, that God was watching you and afterwards you didn't think about it any more, you were all creamy with tenderness and then there were words dancing in your ears: mama, MAMA, MAMA. That only lasted an instant, of course, it was like Lucien trying to balance a chair on his feet. But if, at that moment, you said, "Pacota," God had lost: He had only seen Good and what he saw engraved itself in His memory forever. But Lucien tired of this game because he had to make too much effort and besides you never knew whether God had won or lost. Lucien had nothing more to do with God. When he made his first communion, the curé said he was the best behaved little boy and the most pious of all the catechism class. Lucien grasped things quickly and he had a good memory but his head was full of fog.

Sundays were a bright spot. The fog lifted when Lucien went walking with his father on the Paris road. He had on his handsome sailor suit and they met workers who saluted papa and Lucien. Papa went up to them and they said, "Good morning, M. Fleurier," and also, "Good morning, Master Fleurier." Lucien liked the workers because they were grown-ups but not like the others. First, they called him master. And they wore caps and had short nails and big hands which always looked chapped and hurt. They were responsible and respectful. You mustn't pull old Bouligaud's moustache: papa would have scolded Lucien. But when he spoke to papa, old Bouligaud took off his cap and papa and Lucien kept their hats on and papa spoke in a loud voice, smiling and somewhat testy. "So, we're waiting for our boy, are we, Bouligaud? When does he get leave?" "At the end of the month, Monsieur Fleurier, thank you, Monsieur Fleurier." Old Bouligaud looked happy and he wasn't allowed to slap Lucien on the rear and call him Toad, like M. Bouffardier. Lucien hated M. Bouffardier because he was so ugly. But when he saw old Bouligaud he felt all tender and wanted to be good. Once, coming back from the walk, papa took Lucien on his knees and explained to him what it was to be a boss. Lucien wanted to know how papa talked to the workers when he was at the factory and papa showed him how you had to do it and his voice was all changed. "Will I be a boss too?" Lucien asked. "Yes, indeed, my little man, that's what I made you for." "And who will I command?" "Well, when I'm dead you'll be the boss of my factory and you'll command my workers." "But they'll be dead too." "Well, you'll command their children and you must know how to make yourself obeyed and liked." "And how will I make myself be liked, papa?" Papa thought a little and said, "First, you must know them all by name." Lucien was deeply touched and when the foreman Morel's son came to the house to announce that his father had two fingers cut off, Lucien spoke seriously and gently with him, looking him straight in the eye and calling him Morel. Mama said she was proud to have such a good, sensitive little boy. After that came the armistice, papa read the papers aloud every evening, everybody was talking about the Russians and the German government and reparations and papa showed Lucien the countries on the map: Lucien spent the most boring year of his life, he liked it better when the war was still going on; now everybody looked lost and the light you saw in Mme. Coffin's eyes went out. In October, 1919, Mme. Fleurier made him attend the Ecole Saint-Joseph as a day student.

It was hot in Abbé Geromet's office. Lucien was standing near the abbé's armchair, he had his hands clasped behind him and was deeply bored. "Isn't mama going to go soon?" But Mme. Fleurier had not yet thought of leaving. She was seated on the very edge of a green armchair and stretched out her ample bosom to the abbé; she spoke quickly and she had her musical voice she used when she was angry and didn't want to show it. The abbé spoke slowly and the words seemed much longer in his mouth than in other people's, you might think he was sucking them the way you suck barley sugar before swallowing it. He explained to mama that Lucien was a good little boy and polite and a good worker but so terribly indifferent to everything and Mme. Fleurier said that she was very disappointed because she thought a change would do him good. She asked if he played, at least, during recess. "Alas, madame," the old priest answered, "even games do not seem to interest him. He is sometimes turbulent and even violent but he tires quickly; I believe he lacks perseverance." Lucien thought: they're talking about me. They were two grownups and he was the subject of their conversation, just like the war, the German government or M. Poincaré; they looked serious and they reasoned out his case. But even this thought did not please him. His ears were full of his mother's little singing words, the sucked and sticky words of the abbé, he wanted to cry. Luckily the bell rang and they let him go. But during geography class he felt enervated and asked Abbé Jacquin permission to leave the room because he needed to move around.

First, the coolness, the solitude and the good smell of the toilet calmed him. He squatted down simply to clear his conscience but he didn't feel like it; he raised his head and began reading the inscriptions which covered the door. Someone had written in blue pencil *Barataud is a louse.* Lucien smiled: it was true, Barataud was a louse, he was small and they said he'd grow a little but not much because his father was little, almost a dwarf. Lucien wondered if Barataud had read this inscription and he thought not: otherwise it would be rubbed out. Barataud would have wet his finger and rubbed the letters until they disappeared. Lucien rejoiced a little imagining that Barataud would go to the toilet around four o'clock and that he would take down his velvet pants and read *Barataud is a louse.* Maybe he had never thought he was so small . . . Lucien promised himself to call him a louse starting the next day at recess. He got up on the right hand wall, read another inscription written in the same blue pencil: *Lucien Fleurier is a big beanpole.* He wiped it out carefully and went back to class. It's true, he thought, looking around at his schoolmates, they're all smaller than I am. He felt uncomfortable. Big beanpole. He was sitting at his little desk of holly-wood. Germaine was in the kitchen, mama hadn't come home yet. He wrote "big beanstalk" on a sheet of white paper to re-establish the spelling. But the words seemed too well known and made no effect on him. He called, "Germaine! Germaine!" "What do you want now?" Germaine asked. "Germaine, I'd like you to write on this paper: Lucien Fleurier is a big beanpole." "Have you gone out of your mind, Monsieur Lucien?" He put his arms around her neck. "Be nice, Germaine." Germaine began to laugh and wiped her fat fingers on her apron. He did not look while she was writing, but afterwards he carried the paper to his room and studied it for a long time. Germaine's writing was pointed, Lucien thought he heard a dry voice saying in his ear: big beanpole. He thought, "I'm big." He was crushed with shame: big as Barataud was small and the others laughed behind his back. It was as if someone had cast a spell over him: until then it had seemed natural to see his friends from above. But now it seemed he had been suddenly condemned to be big for the rest of his life. That evening he asked his father if a person could shrink if he wanted to with all his might. M. Fleurier said no: all the Fleuriers had been big and strong and Lucien would grow still bigger. Lucien was without hope. After his mother tucked him in he got up and went to look at himself in the mirror. "I'm big." But he looked in vain, he could not see it, he seemed neither big nor little. He lifted up his nightshirt a little and saw his legs; then he imagined

Costil saying to Hebrard: Say, look at those long beanpoles, and it made him feel funny. He was cold, he shivered and someone said, the beanpole has gooseflesh! Lucien lifted his shirt-tail very high and they all saw his naval and his whole business and then he ran and slipped into bed. When he put his hand under his shirt he thought that Costil saw him and was saying, Look what the big beanpole's doing! He squirmed and turned in bed, breathing heavily. Big beanpole! Big beanpole! until he made a little acid itching come beneath his fingers.

The following days, he wanted to ask the abbé's permission to sit in the rear of the class. It was because of Boisset, Winckelmann and Costil who were behind him and could look at the back of his neck. Lucien felt the back of his neck but he could not see it and often even forgot about it. But while he was answering the abbé as well as he could and was reciting the tirade from *Don Diego,* the others were behind him watching the back of his neck." Lucien forced himself to make his voice swell and express the humiliation of Don Diego. He could do what he wanted with his voice; but the back of his neck was always there, peaceful, inexpressive, like someone resting and Boisset saw it. He dared not change his seat because the last row was reserved for the dunces, but the back of his neck and his shoulder blades were constantly itching and he was obliged to scratch unceasingly. Lucien invented a new game: in the morning, when he took his bath, he imagined someone was watching him through the keyhole, sometimes Costil, sometimes old Bouligaud, sometimes Germaine. Then he turned all around for them to see him from all sides and sometimes he turned his rear toward the door, going down on all fours so that it would look all plump and ridiculous; M. Bouffardier was coming on tiptoe to give him an enema. One day when he was in the bathroom he heard sounds; it was Germaine rubbing polish on the buffet in the hall. His heart stopped beating, he opened the door quietly and went out, his trousers round his heels, his shirt rolled up around his back. He was obliged to make little hops in order to go forward without losing his balance. Germaine looked at him calmly: "What are you doing, running a sack race?" she asked. Enraged, he pulled up his trousers and ran and threw himself on his bed. Mme. Fleurier was heartbroken. She often told her husband, "He was so graceful when he was little and now look how awkward he is, if that isn't a shame." M. Fleurier glanced carelessly at Lucien and answered "It's his age." Lucien did not know what to do with his body; no matter what he did, he felt this body existing on all sides at once, without consulting him. Lucien indulged himself by imagining he was invisible and then he took the habit of looking through keyholes to see how the others were made without their knowing it. He saw his mother while she was washing. She was seated on the *bidet,* she seemed asleep and she had surely forgotten her body and her face, because she thought that no one saw her. The sponge went back and forth by itself over this abandoned flesh; she moved lazily and he felt she was going to stop somewhere along the way. Mama rubbed a washcloth with a piece of soap and her hand disappeared between her legs. Her face was restful, almost sad, surely she was thinking of something else, about Lucien's education or M. Poincaré. But during this time she *was* this gross pink mass, this voluminous body hanging over the porcelain *bidet.* Another time, Lucien removed his shoes and climbed all the way up to the eaves. He saw Germaine. She had on a long green chemise which fell to her feet, she was combing her hair before a small round mirror and she smiled softly at her image. Lucien began to laugh uncontrolledly and had to climb down hurriedly. After that he smiled and made faces at himself in front of the mirror in the salon and after a moment was seized with terrible fears.

Lucien finally went completely asleep but no one noticed except Mme. Coffin who called him her sleeping beauty; a great air bubble he could neither swallow nor spit out was always in his half open mouth: it was his *yawning;* when he was alone the bubble grew larger, caressing his palate and tongue; his mouth opened wide and tears ran down his cheeks: these were very pleasant moments. He did not amuse himself as much in the bathroom but to make up for it he liked very much to sneeze, it woke him up and for an instant he looked around him, exhilarated, then dozed off again. He learned to recognize different sorts of sleep: in winter, he sat before the fireplace and stretched his head toward the blaze; when it was quite red and roasted it suddenly emptied; he called that "head sleeping." Sunday morning, on the other hand, he went to sleep by the feet: he got into his bath, slowly lowered himself and sleep climbed in ripples all along his legs and thighs. Above the sleeping body, all white and swollen like a stewed chicken at the bottom of the water, a little blond head was enthroned, full of wise words, templum, templi, templo, iconoclasts. In class sleep was white and riddled with flashes: First: Lucien Fleurier. "What was the third estate?

Nothing." First, Lucien Fleurier, second, Winckelmann, Pellereau was first in algebra; he had only one testicle, the other one hadn't come down; he made them pay two sous to see and ten to touch. Lucien gave the ten sous, hesitated, stretched out his hand and left without touching, but afterwards his regrets were so great that sometimes they kept him awake for more than an hour. He was less good in geology than in history. First, Winckelmann, second, Fleurier. On Sundays he went bicycling with Costil and Winckelmann. Through russet, heat-crushed countrysides, the bicycles skidded in the marrowy dust; Lucien's legs were active and muscular but the sleepy odor of the roads went to his head, he bent over the handlebars, his eyes grew pink and half closed. He won the honor prize three times in a row. They gave him *Fabiola, or The Church in the Catacombs,* the *Genie du Christianisme* and the *Life of Cardinal Lavigerie.* Costil, back from the long vacation, taught them all *De Profondis Morpionibus* and the *Artilleur de Metz.* Lucien decided to do better and consulted his father's *Larousse Medical Dictionary* on the article "Uterus," then he explained to them how women were made, he even made a sketch on the board and Costil declared it disgusting; but after that they could hear no mention of "tubes" without bursting out laughing and Lucine thought with satisfaction that in all of France you coudn't find a second class student and perhaps even a rhetoric student who knew female organs as well as he.

It was like a flash of magnesium when the Fleuriers moved to Paris. Lucien could no longer sleep because of the movies, cars and streets. He learned to distinguish a Voisin from a Packard, a Hispano-Suiza from a Rolls and he spoke frequently of cars. He had been wearing long pants for more than a year. His father sent him to England as a reward for his success in the first part of the baccalaureat; Lucien saw plains swollen with water and white cliffs, he boxed with John Latimer and learned the overarm stroke but, one fine day, he woke up to find himself asleep, it had come back; he went somnolently back to Paris. The elementary mathematics class in the Lycée Condorcet had 37 pupils. Eight of these pupils said they knew all about women and called the others virgins. The Enlightened scorned Lucien until the first of November, but on All Saint's Day, Lucien went walking with Garry, the most experienced of all of them and negligently showed him proof of such anatomical knowledge that Garry was astonished. Lucien did not enter the group of the enlightened because his parents did not allow him out at night, but he had a deeper and deeper understanding.

On Thursday, Aunt Berthe and Riri came to lunch at Rue Raynouard. She had grown enormous and sad and spent her time sighing; but since her skin had remained very fine and white, Lucien would have liked to see her naked. He thought about it that night in bed; it would be a winter day, in the Bois de Boulogne, he would come upon her naked in a copse, her arms crossed on her breast, shivering with gooseflesh. He imagined that a nearsighted passer-by touched her with his cane and said, "Well, what can that be?" Lucien did not get along too well with his cousin: Riri had become a very handsome young man, a little too elegant. He was taking philosophy at Lakanal and understood nothing of mathematics. Lucien could not keep himself from thinking that Riri, seven years ago, still did number two in his pants and after that walked with his legs wide apart like a duck and looked at his mother with candid eyes saying, "No, mama, I didn't do it, I promise." And he had some repugnance about touching Riri's hand. Yet he was very nice to him and explained his mathematics courses; sometimes he had to make a great effort not to lose patience because Riri was not very intelligent. But he never let himself be carried away and always kept a calm, poised voice. Mme. Fleurier thought Lucien had much tact but Aunt Berthe showed him no gratitude. When Lucien proposed to give Riri a lesson she blushed a little, moved about on her chair, saying, "No, you're very kind, my little Lucien, but Riri is too big a boy. He can if he wants; but he must not get in the habit of counting on others." One night Mme. Fleurier told Lucien brusquely, "You think Riri's grateful for what you're doing for him? Well, don't kid yourself, my boy: he thinks you're stuck-up, your Aunt Berthe told me so." She had assumed her musical voice and familiar air; Lucien realized she was mad with rage. He felt vaguely intrigued but could find nothing to answer. The next day and the day after that he had a lot of work and the whole episode left his mind.

Sunday morning he set his pen down brusquely and wondered, "Am I stuck-up?" It was eleven o'clock; sitting in his study Lucien watched the pink cretonne designs of the cretons which lined the walls; on his left cheek he felt the dry and dusty warmth of the first April sunlight, on his right cheek he felt the heavy, stifling heat of the radiator. "Am I stuck-up?" It was hard to answer. Lucien first tried to remember his last conversation with Riri and to judge his own attitude impartially. He had bent over Riri and smiled at him, saying, "You get it? If you don't catch on, don't be afraid to say so, and we'll start over." A little later he had made an error in a delicate problem and said, gaily, "That's one on me." It was an expression he had taken from M. Fleurier which amused him: "But was I stuck-up when I said that?" By dint of searching, he suddenly made something round and white appear, soft as a bit of cloud: it was his thought of the other day: he had said, "Do you get it?" and it was in his head but it couldn't be described. Lucien made desperate efforts to *look* at this bit of cloud and he suddenly felt as though he were falling into it head first, he found himself in the mist and became mist himself, he was no more than a damp white warmth which smelled of linen. He wanted to tear himself from this mist and come back but it came with him. He thought, "I'm Lucien Fleurier, I'm in my room, I'm doing a problem in physics, it's Sunday." But his thoughts melted into banks of white fog. He shook himself and began counting the cretonne characters, two shepherdesses, two shepherds and Cupid. Then suddenly he told himself, "I am . . ." and there was a slight click: he had awakened from his long somnolence.

It was not pleasant. The shepherds had jumped back, it seemed to Lucien that he was looking at them from the wrong end of a telescope. In place of his stupor so sweet to him and which lost itself in its own folds, there was now a small, wide-awake perplexity which wondered, "Who am I?"

"Who am I? I look at the bureau, I look at the notebook. My name is Lucien Fleurier but that's only a name. I'm stuck-up. I'm not stuck-up. I don't know, but it doesn't make sense."

"I'm a good student. No. That's a lie: a good student likes to work—not me. I have good marks but I don't like to work. I don't hate it, either, I don't give a damn. I don't give a damn about anything. I'll never be a boss." He thought with anguish "But what will I be?" A moment passed; he scratched his cheek and shut his left eye because the sun was in it: "What am I, I . . . ?" There was this fog rolling back on itself, indefinite. "I!" He looked into the distance; the word rang in his head and then perhaps it was possible to make out something, like the top of a pyramid whose side vanished, far off, into the fog. Lucien shuddered and his hands trembled. "Now I have it!" he thought, "now I have it! I was sure of it: *I don't exist!*"

During the months that followed, Lucien often tried to go

back to sleep but did not succeed: he slept well and regularly nine hours a night and the rest of the time was more lively and more and more perplexed: his parents said he had never been so healthy. When he happened to think he did not have the stuff to make a boss he felt romantic and wanted to walk for hours under the moon; but his parents still did not allow him out at night. Often, then, he would stretch out on his bed and take his temperature: the thermometer showed 98.6 or 98.7 and Lucien thought with bitter pleasure that his parents found him looking fine. "I don't exist." He closed his eyes and let himself drift: existence is an illusion because I *know* I don't exist, all I have to do is plug my ears and not think about anything and I'll become nothingness." But the illusion was tenacious. Over other people, at least, he had the malicious superiority of possessing a secret: Garry, for instance, didn't exist any more than Lucien. But it was enough to see him snorting tempestuously in the midst of his admirers: you could see right away he thought his own existence as solid as iron. Neither did M. Fleurier exist— nor Riri—nor anyone—the world was a comedy without actors. Lucien, who had been given an "A" for his dissertation on "Morality and Science," dreamed of writing a "Treatise on Nothingness" and he imagined that people, reading it, would disappear one after the other like vampires at cockcrow. Before beginning this treatise, he wanted the advice of The Baboon, his philosophy prof. "Excuse me, sir," he said at the end of a class, "could anyone claim that we don't exist?" The Baboon said no. "Goghito," he said, "ergo zum. You exist because you doubt your existence." Lucien was not convinced but he gave up his work. In July, he was given, without fanfare, his baccalaureat in mathematics and left for Férolles with his parents. The perplexity still did not leave him: it was like wanting to sneeze.

Old Bouligaud had died and the mentality of M. Fleurier's workers had changed a lot. Now they were drawing large salaries and their wives bought silk stockings. Mme. Bouffardier cited frightful examples to Mme. Fleurier: "My maid tells me she saw that little Ansiaume girl in the cook-shop. She's the daughter of one of your husband's best workers, the one we took care of when she lost her mother. She married a fitter from Beaupertuis. Well, she ordered a 20-franc chicken. And so arrogant! Nothing's good enough for them: they want to have everything we have." Now, when Lucien took short Sunday walks with his father, the workers barely touched their caps on seeing them and there were even some who crossed over so as not to salute them. One day Lucien met Bouligaud's son who did not even seem to recognize him. Lucien was a little excited about it: here was a chance to prove himself a boss. He threw an eagle eye on Jules Bouligaud and went toward him, his hands behind his back. But Bouligaud did not seem intimidated: he turned vacant eyes to Lucien and passed by him, whistling. "He didn't recognize me," Lucien told himself. But he was deeply disappointed and, in the following days, thought more than ever that the world did not exist.

Mme. Fleurier's little revolver was put away in the left-hand drawer of her dressing table. Her husband made her a present of it in September, 1914, before he left for the front. Lucien took it and turned it around in his hand for a long while: it was a little jewel, with a gilded barrel and a butt inlaid with mother of pearl. He could not rely on a philosophical treatise to persuade people they did not exist. Action was needed, a really desperate act which would dissolve appearances and show the nothingness of the world in full light. A shot, a young body bleeding on the carpet, a few words scribbled on a piece of paper: "I kill myself because I do not exist. And you too, my brothers, you are nothingness!" People would read the newspaper in the morning and would see "An adolescent has dared!" And each would feel himself terribly troubled and would wonder, "And what about me? Do I exist?" There had been similar epidemics of suicide in history, among others after the publication of Werther. Lucien thought how "martyr" in Greek meant "witness." He was too sensitive for a boss but not for a martyr. As a result, he often entered his mother's room and looked at the revolver; he was filled with agony. Once he even bit the gilded barrel, gripping his fingers tightly around the butt. The rest of the time he was very gay for he thought that all true leaders had known the temptation of suicide. Napoleon, for example. Lucien did not hide from himself the fact that he was touching the depths of despair but he hoped to leave this crisis with a tempered soul and he read the *Mémorial de Saint-Hélène* with interest. Yet he had to make a decision: Lucien set September 30 as the end of his hesitations. The last days were extremely difficult: surely the crisis was salutary, but it required of Lucien a tension so strong that he thought he would break, one day, like a glass. He no longer dared to touch the revolver; he contented himself with opening the drawer, lifting up his mother's slips a little and studying at great length the icy, headstrong little monster which rested in a hollow of pink silk. Yet he felt a sharp disappointment when he decided to live and found himself completely unoccupied. Fortunately, the multiple cares of going back to school absorbed him: his parents sent him to the Lycée Saint-Louis to take prepartory courses for the Ecole Centrale. He wore a fine red-bordered cap with an insignia and sang:

> C'est le piston qui fait marcher les machines
> C'est le piston qui fait marcher les wagons . . .

This new dignity of *piston* filled Lucien with pride; and then his class was not like the others: it had traditions and a ceremonial; it was a force. For instance, it was the usual thing at the end of the French class for a voice to ask,"What's a *cyrard?*" and everybody answered softly, "A *con!*" After which the voice repeated, "What's an *agro?*" and they answered a little louder, "A *con!*" Then M. Béthune, who was almost blind and wore dark glasses, said wearily, "Please, gentlemen!" There were a few moments of absolute silence and the students looked at each other with smiles of intelligence, then someone shouted, "What's a *piston?*" and they all roared, "A great man!" At those times Lucien felt galvanized. In the evening he told his parents the various incidents of the day in great detail and when he said, "Then the whole class started laughing . . ." or "the whole class decided to put Meyrinez in quarantine," the words, in passing, warmed his mouth like a drink of liquor. Yet the first months were very hard: Lucien missed his math and physics and then, individually, his schoolmates were not too sympathetic: they were on scholarships, mostly grinds, untidy and ill-mannered. "There isn't one," he told his father, "I could make a friend of." "Young men on scholarships," M. Fleurier said dreamily, "represent an intellectual elite and yet they're poor leaders: they have missed one thing." Hearing him talk about "poor leaders," Lucien felt a disagreeable pinching in his heart and again thought of killing himself during the weeks that followed, but he had not the same enthusiasm as he had during vacation. In January, a new student named Berliac scandalized the whole class: he wore coats ringed in green or purple, in the latest styles, little round collars and trousers that are seen in tailors' engravings, so narrow that one wondered how he could even get into them. From the beginning, he was classed last in mathematics. "I don't give a damn," he said, "I'm literary, I take math to mortify myself." After a month he had won everyone's heart: he distributed contraband cigarettes and told them he had women and showed letters they sent him. The whole class decided he was all right and it would be best to let him alone. Lucien greatly admired his elegance and manners, but Berliac treated Lucien with condescension and called him a "rich kid." "After all," Lucien said one day, "it's better than being a poor kid." Berliac smiled. "You're a little cynic!" he told him and the next day he let him read one of his poems: "Caruso gobbled raw eyes every evening, otherwise he was sober as a camel. A lady made a bouquet with the eyes of her family and threw it on the stage. Everyone bows before this exemplary gesture. But do not forget that her hour of glory lasts only 27 minutes: precisely from the first bravo to the extinction of the great chandelier in the Opera (after that she must keep her husband on a leash, winner of several contests, who filled the pink cavities of his orbits with two croix-de-guerre). And note well: all those among us who eat too much canned human flesh shall perish with scurvy." "It's very good," Lucien said, taken aback— "I get them by a new technique called automatic writing." Some time later Lucien had a violent desire to kill himself and decided to ask Berliac's advice. "What must I do?" he asked after he had explained the case. Berliac listened attentively; he was in the habit of sucking his fingers and then coating the pimples on his face with saliva, so that his skin glistened in spots like a road after a rainstorm. "Do what you want," he said, "it makes absolutely no difference." Lucien was a little disappointed but he realized Berliac had been profoundly touched when he asked Lucien to have tea with his mother the next Thursday. Mme. Berliac was very friendly; she had warts and a wine-colored birthmark on her left cheek: "You see," Berliac told Lucien, "we are the real victims of the war." That was also the opinion of Lucien and they agreed that they both belonged to the same sacrificed generation. Night fell, Berliac was lying on his bed, his hands knotted behind his head. They smoked English cigarettes, played phonograph records and Lucien heard the voice of Sophie Tucker and Al Jolson. They grew melancholy and Lucien thought Berliac was his best friend. Berliac asked him if he knew about psychoanalysis; his voice was serious and he looked at Lucien with gravity. "I desired my mother until I was fifteen," he confided. Lucien felt uncomfortable; he was afraid of blushing and remembered Mme. Berliac's moles and could not understand how anyone could desire her. Yet when she came to bring them toast, he was vaguely troubled and tried to imagine her breasts through the yellow sweater she wore. When she left, Berliac said in a positive voice, "Naturally, you've wanted to sleep with your mother too." He did not question, he affirmed. Lucien shrugged. "Naturally," he said. The next day he was worried, he was afraid Berliac would repeat their conversation. But he reassured himself quickly: After all, he thought, he's compromised himself more than I. He was quite taken by the scientific turn their confidences had taken and on the following Thursday he read a book on dreams by Freud he found in the Sainte-Geneviève Library. It was a revelation. "So that's it," Lucien repeated, roaming the streets, "so that's it." Next he bought *Introduction to Psychoanalysis* and *Psychopathology of Everyday Life,* and everything became clear to him. This strange feeling of not existing, this long emptiness in his conscience, his somnolence, his perplexities, his vain efforts to know himself which met only a curtain of fog . . . "My God," he thought, "I have a complex." He told Berliac how he was when he was a child, imagining he was a sleepwalker and how objects never seemed quite real to him. "I must have," he concluded, "a very extraordinary complex." "Just like me," said Berliac, "we both have terrific complexes!" They got the habit of interpreting their dreams and their slightest gestures; Berliac always had so many stories to tell that Lucien suspected him of inventing them, or at least enlarging them. But they got along well and approached the most delicate subjects with objectivity; they confessed to each other that they wore a mask of gaiety to deceive their associates but at heart were terribly tormented. Lucien was freed from his worries. He threw himself greedily into psychoanalysis because he realized it was something that agreed with him and now he felt reassured, he no longer needed to worry or to be always searching his conscience for palpable manifestations of his character. The true Lucien was deeply buried in his subconscious; he had to dream of him without ever seeing him, as an absent friend. All day Lucien thought of his complexes and with a certain pride he imagined the obscure world, cruel and violent, that rumbled beneath the mists of his consciousness. "You understand," he told Berliac, "in appearance I was a sleepy kid, indifferent to everything, somebody not too interesting. And even inside, you know, it seemed to be so much like that that I almost let myself be caught. But I knew there was something else." "There's *always* something else," Berliac answered. They smiled proudly at each other, Lucien wrote a poem called "When the Fog Lifts" and Berliac found it excellent, but he reproached

Lucien for having written it in regular verse. Still, they learned it by heart and when they wished to speak of their libidos they said willingly:

"The great crabs wrapped in the mantle of fog," then simply, "crabs," winking an eye. But after a while, Lucien, when he was alone at night, began to find all that a little terrifying. He no longer dared look his mother in the face and when he kissed her before going to bed he was afraid some shadowy power would deviate his kiss and drop it on Mme. Fleurier's mouth, it was as if he carried a volcano within himself. Lucien treated himself with caution in order not to violate the sumptuous, sinister soul he had discovered. Now he knew the price of everything and dreaded the terrible awakening. "I'm afraid of myself," he said. For six months he had renounced solitary practices because they annoyed him and he had too much work but he returned to them: everyone had to follow their bent, the books of Freud were filled with stories of unfortunate young people who became neurotic because they broke too quickly with their habits. "Are we going to go crazy?" he asked Berliac. And in fact, on certain Thursdays they felt strange; shadows had cunningly slipped into Berliac's room, they smoked whole packs of scented cigarettes, and their hands trembled. Then one of them would rise without a word, tiptoe to the door and turn the switch. A yellow light flooded the room and they looked at each other with defiance.

Lucien was not late in noticing that his friendship with Berliac was based on a misunderstanding; surely no one was more sensitive than he to the pathetic beauty of the Oedipus complex but in it he saw especially the sign of a power for passion which later he would like to use toward different ends. On the other hand, Berliac seemed to be content with his state and had no desire to leave it. "We're screwed," he said proudly, "We're flops. We'll never do anything." "Never anything." Lucien answered in echo. But he was furious. After Easter vacation Berliac told him he had shared his mother's room in a hotel in Dijon: he had risen very early in the morning, went to the bed on which his mother still was sleeping and gently lifted up the covers. "Her nightgown was up," he grinned. Hearing these words, Lucien could not keep himself from scorning Berliac a little and he felt quite alone. It was fine to have complexes but you had to know how to get rid of them eventually. How would a man be able to assume responsibilities and take command if he still had an infantile sexuality? Lucien began to worry seriously: he would have liked to take the advice of some competent person but he did not know whom to see. Berliac often spoke to him about a surrealist named Bergère who was well versed in psychoanalysis and who seemed to have a great ascendancy over him; but he had never offered to introduce him to Lucien. Lucien was also very disappointed because he had counted on Berliac to get women for him; he thought that the possession of a pretty mistress would naturally change the course of his ideas. But Berliac spoke no more of his lady friends. Sometimes they went along the boulevards and followed women, never daring to speak to them: "What do you expect, old man?" Berliac said. "We aren't the kind that pleases. Women feel something frightening in us." Lucien did not answer; Berliac began to annoy him. He often made jokes in very bad taste about Lucien's parents, he called them M. and Mme. Dumollet. Lucien understood very well that a surrealist scorned the bourgeoisie in general, but Berliac had been invited several times by Mme. Fleurier who had treated him with confidence and friendship: lacking gratitude, a simple attention to decency would have kept him from speaking of her in that manner. And then Berliac was terrible with his mania for borrowing money and never returning it, in a café he only proposed to pay the round once out of five. Lucien told him plainly one day that he didn't understand, and that between friends, they should share all expenses. Berliac looked at him deeply and said, "I thought so: you're an anal," and he explained the Freudian relation to him; feces equal gold and the Freudian theory of guilt. "I'd like to know one thing," he said, "until what age did your mother wipe you?" They almost fought.

From the beginning of May, Berliac began to cut school: Lucien went to meet him after class, in a bar on Rue des Petits-Champs where they drank Crucifix Vermouths. One Tuesday afternoon Lucien found Berliac sitting in front of an empty glass. "Oh, there you are," Berliac said. "Listen, I've got to beat it, I have an appointment with the dentist at five. Wait for me, he lives near here and it'll only take a half hour." "OK," Lucien answered, dropping into a chair. "François, give me a white vermouth." Just then a man came into the bar and smiled surprisedly at seeing them. Berliac blushed and got up hurriedly. "Who can that be?" Lucien wondered. Berliac, shaking hands with the stranger, stood so as to hide Lucien; he spoke in a low, rapid voice, the other answered clearly, "Indeed not, my friend, you'll always be a fool." At the same time he raised himself on tiptoe and looked at Lucien over Berliac's head with calm assurance. He could have been 35; he had a pale face and magnificent white hair: "It's surely Bergère," Lucien thought, his heart pounding, "how handsome he is."

Berliac had taken the man with white hair by the elbow with an air of timid authority.

"Come with me," he said, "I'm going to the dentist, just across the way."

"But you were with a friend, weren't you?" the other answered, his eyes not leaving Lucien's face. "You should introduce us."

Lucien got up, smiling, "Caught!" he thought; his cheeks were burning. Berliac's neck disappeared into his shoulders and for a second Lucien thought he was going to refuse. "So introduce me," he said gaily. But as soon as he had spoken the blood rushed to his temples and he wished the ground would swallow him. Berliac turned around and without looking at anyone, muttered "Lucien Fleurier, a friend from the lycée, Monsieur Achille Bergère."

"I admire your works," Lucien said feebly. Bergère took his hand in his own long, delicate fingers and motioned him to sit down. Bergère enveloped Lucien with a tender, warm look; he was still holding his hand. "Are you worried?" he asked gently.

"I am worried," he answered distinctly. It seemed he had just undergone the trials of an initiation. Berliac hesitated an instant then angrily sat down again, throwing his hat on the table. Lucien burned with a desire to tell Bergère of his attempted suicide; this was someone to whom one had to speak of things abruptly and without preparation. He dared not say anything because of Berliac; he hated Berliac.

"Do you have any *raki*?" Bergère asked the waiter.

"No, they don't," Berliac said quickly; "It's a nice little place but all they have to drink is vermouth."

"What's that yellow stuff you have in the bottle?" Bergère asked with an ease full of softness.

"White Crucifix," the waiter answered.

"All right, I'll have some of that."

Berliac squirmed on his chair: he seemed caught between a desire to show off his friends and the fear of making Lucien shine at his expense. Finally, he said, in a proud and dismal voice, "He wanted to kill himself."

"My God!" Bergère said, "I should hope so!"

There was another silence: Lucien had lowered his eyes modestly but he wondered if Berliac wasn't soon going to clear out: Bergère suddenly looked at his watch. "What about your dentist?" he asked.

Berliac rose ungraciously. "Come with me, Bergère," he begged, "it isn't fair."

"No, you'll be back. I'll keep your friend company."

Berliac stayed for another moment, shifting from one foot to the other.

"Go on," Bergère said imperiously, "You'll meet us here."

When Berliac had gone, Bergère got up and sat next to Lucien. Lucien told him of his suicide at great length; he also explained to him that he had desired his mother and that he was a sadico-anal and that fundamentally he didn't love anything and that everything in him was a comedy. Bergère listened without a word, watching him closely and Lucien found it delicious to be understood. When he finished, Bergère passed his arm familiarly around his shoulders and Lucien smelled a scent of eau-de-cologne and English tobacco.

"Do you know, Lucien, how I would describe your condition?" Lucien looked at Bergère hopefully; he was not disappointed.

"I call it," Bergère said, "disorder."

Disorder: the word had begun tender and white as moonlight but the final "order" had the coppered flash of a trumpet.

"Disorder," Lucien said.

He felt as grave and uneasy as the time he told Riri he was a sleepwalker. The bar was dark but the door opened wide on the street, on the luminous springtime mist; under the discreet perfume Bergère gave off, Lucien perceived the heavy odor of the obscure room, an odor of red wine and damp wood. "Disorder," he thought; what good will that do me? He did not know whether a dignity or new sickness had been discovered in him; near his eyes he saw the quick lips of Bergère veiling and unveiling incessantly the sparkle of a gold tooth.

"I like people in disorder," Bergère said, "and I think you are extraordinarily lucky. For after all, that has been given you. You see all these swine? They're pedestrian. You'd have to give them to the red ants to stir them up a little. Do you know they have the consciousness of beasts?"

"They eat men," Lucien said.

"Yes, they strip skeletons of the human meat."

"I see," Lucien said. He added, "And I? What must I do?"

"Nothing, for God's sake," Bergère said with a look of comic fear. "Above all, don't sit down. Unless," he said laughing, "it's on a tack. Have you read Rimbaud?"

"N-no," Lucien said.

"I'll lend you *The Illuminations*. Listen, we must see each other again. If you're free Thursday, stop in and see me around 3, I live in Montparnasse, 9 Rue Campagne-Première."

The next Thursday Lucien went to see Bergère and he went back almost every day throughout May. They agreed to tell Berliac that they saw each other once a week, because they wanted to be frank with him and yet avoid hurting his feelings. Berliac showed himself to be completely out of sorts; he asked Lucien, grinning, "So, are you going steady? He gave you the worry business and you gave him the suicide business: a great game, what?" Lucien protested, "I'd like to have you know that it was you who talked about my suicide first." "Oh," Berliac said, "it was only to spare you the shame of telling it yourself." Their meetings became more infrequent. "Everything I liked about him," Lucien told Bergère one day, "he borrowed from you, I realize it now." "Berliac is a monkey," Bergère said, laughing, "that's what always attracted me. Did you know his maternal grandmother was a Jewess? That explains a lot of things." "Rather," Lucien answered. After an instant he added, "Besides, he's very charming." Bergère's apartment was filled with strange and comical objects: hassocks whose red velvet seats rested on the legs of painted wooden women, Negro statuettes, a studded chastity belt of forged iron, plaster breasts in which little spoons had been planted, on the desk a gigantic bronze louse and a monk's skull stolen from the Mistra Ossuary served as paper weights. The walls were papered with notices announcing the death of the surrealist Bergère. In spite of all this, the apartment gave the impression of intelligent comfort and Lucien liked to stretch out on the deep divan in the den. What particularly surprised Lucien was the enormous quantity of practical jokes Bergère had accumulated on a shelf: solid liquids, sneezing powder, itching powder, floating sugar, an imitation turd and a bride's garter. While Bergère spoke, he took the artificial turd between his fingers and considered it with gravity. "These jokes," he said, "have a revolutionary value. They disturb. There is more destructive power in them than in all the works of Lenin." Lucien, surprised and charmed, looked by turns at this handsome tormented face with hollow eyes and these long delicate fingers gracefully holding a perfectly imitated excrement. Bergère spoke often of Rimbaud and the "systematic disordering of all the senses." "When you will be able, in crossing the Place de la Concorde, to see distinctly and at will a kneeling Negress sucking the obelisk, you will be able to tell yourself that you have torn down the scenery and you are saved." He lent him *The Illuminations*, the *Chants de Maldoror* and the works of the Marquis de Sade. Lucien tried conscientiously to understand them, but many things escaped him and he was shocked because Rimbaud was a pederast. He told Bergère who began to laugh. "Why not, my little friend?" Lucien was very embarrassed. He blushed and for a minute began to hate Bergère with all his might, but he mastered it, raised his head and said with simple frankness, "I'm talking nonsense." Bergère stroked his hair; he seemed moved; "These great eyes full of trouble," he said, "these doe's eyes. . . . Yes, Lucien, you talked nonsense. Rimbaud's pederasty is the first and genial disordering of his sensitivity. We owe his poems to it. To think that there are specific objects of sexual desire and that these objects are women because they have a hole between their legs, is the hideous and wilful error of the pedestrian. Look!" He took from his desk a dozen yellowing photos and threw them on Lucien's knees. Lucien gazed on horrible naked whores, laughing with toothless mouths, spreading their legs like lips and darting between their thighs something like a mossy tongue. "I got the collection for 3 francs at Bou-Saada," Bergère said. "If you kiss the behind of one of those women, you're a regular guy and everybody will say you're a he-man. Because they're women, do you understand? I tell you the first thing to convince yourself of is that *everything* can be an object of sexual desire, a sewing machine, a measuring glass, a horse or a shoe. I," he smiled, "have made love with flies. I know a marine who used to sleep with ducks. He put the head in a drawer, held them firmly by the feet and hoop-la!" Bergère pinched Lucien's ear distractedly and concluded, "The duck died and the battalion ate it." Lucien emerged from these conversations with his face on fire, he thought Bergère was a genius but sometimes he woke up at night, drenched in sweat, his head filled with monstrous obscene visions and he wondered if Bergère was a good influence on him. "To be alone," he cried, wringing his hands, "to have no one to advise me, to tell me if I'm on the right path." If he went to the very end, if he really practiced the disordering of the senses, would he lose his footing and drown? One day Bergère had spoken to him of André Breton; Lucien murmured, as if in a dream, "Yes, but afterwards, if I could never come back." Bergère started. "Come back? Who's talking about coming back? If you go insane, so much the better. After that, as Rimbaud says, *'viendront d'autres horribles travailleurs.'*" "That's what I thought," Lucien said sadly. He had noticed that these long chats had the opposite effect from the one wished for by Bergère: as soon as Lucien caught himself showing the beginnings of a fine sensation or an original impression, he began to tremble: "Now it's starting," he thought. He would willingly have wished to have only the most banal, stupid perception; he only felt comfortable in the evenings with his parents: that was his refuge. They talked about Briand, the bad faith of the Germans, of cousin Jeanne's confinements, and the cost of living; Lucien voluptuously exchanged good common sense with them. One day after leaving Bergère, he was entering his room and mechanically locked the door and slid the bolt. When he noticed this gesture he forced himself to laugh at it but that night he could not sleep: he had just understood he was afraid.

However, nothing in the world would have stopped him from seeing Bergère. "He fascinates me," he told himself. And then he had a lively appreciation of the friendship so delicate and so particular which Bergère had been able to establish between them. Without dropping a virile, almost rude tone of voice, Bergère had the artistry to make Lucien feel, and, in a way of speaking, touch his tenderness: for instance, he re-knotted his tie and scolded him for being so untidy, he combed his hair with a gold comb from Cambodia. He made Lucien discover his own body and explained to him the harsh and pathetic beauty of Youth: "You are Rimbaud," he told him, "he had your big hands when he came to Paris to see Verlaine. He had this pink face of a young healthy peasant and this long slim body of a fair-haired girl." He made Lucien unbutton his collar and open his shirt, then led him, confused, before a mirror and made him admire the charming harmony of his red cheeks and white throat; then he caressed Lucien's hips with a light hand and added, sadly, "We should kill ourselves at twenty." Often now, Lucien looked at himself in mirrors and he learned to enjoy his young awkward grace. "I am Rimbaud," he thought, in the evenings, removing his clothing with gestures full of gentleness and he began to believe that he would have the short and tragic life of a too-beautiful flower. At these times, it seemed to him that he had known, long before, similar impressions and an absurd image came to his mind: he saw himself again, small, with a long blue robe and angel's wings, distributing flowers at a charity sale. He looked at his long legs. "Is it true I have such a soft skin?" he thought with amusement. And once he ran his lips over his forearm from the wrist to the elbow, along a charming blue vein.

One day, he had an unpleasant surprise going to Bergère's: Berliac was there, busy cutting with a knife fragments of a blackish substance that looked like a clod of earth. The two young people had not seen each other for ten days: they shook hands coldly. "See that?" Berliac said, "that's hasheesh. We're going to put it in these pipes, between two layers of light tobacco, it gives a surprising effect. There's some for you," he added. "No thanks," Lucien said, "I don't care for it." The other two laughed and Berliac insisted, looking ugly: "But you're crazy, old man, you've got to take some. You can't imagine how pleasant it is." "I told you no," Lucien said. Berliac said no more, merely smiled with a superior air and Lucien saw Bergère was smiling too. He tapped his foot and said "I don't want any, I don't want to knock myself out, I think it's crazy to stupefy yourself with that stuff." He had let that go in spite of himself, but when he realized the range of what he had just said and imagined what Bergère must think of him, he wanted to kill Berliac and tears came to his eyes. "You're a bourgeois," said Berliac, shrugging his shoulders, "you pretend to swim but you're much too afraid of going out of your depth." "I don't want to get in the drug habit," Lucien said in a calmer voice; "one slavery is like another and I want to stay clear." "Say you're afraid to get into it," Berliac answered violently. Lucien was going to slap him when he heard the imperious voice of Bergère. "Let him alone, Charles," he told Berliac, "he's right. His fear of being involved is *also* disorder." They both smoked, stretched out on the divan and an odor of Armenian paper filled the room. Lucien sat on a red velvet hassock and watched them in silence. After a time, Berliac let his head fall back and fluttered his eyelids with a moist smile. Lucien watched him with rancor and felt humiliated. At last Berliac got up and walked unsteadily out of the room: to the end he had the funny, sleeping and voluptuous smile on his lips. "Give me a pipe," Lucien said hoarsely. Bergère began to laugh. "Don't bother," he said, "don't worry about Berliac. Do you know what he's doing now?" "I don't give a damn," Lucien said. "Well, I'll tell you anyhow. He's vomiting," Bergère said calmly. "That's the only effect hasheesh ever

had on him. The rest is a joke, but I make him smoke it sometimes because he wants to show off and it amuses me." The next
day Berliac came to the lycée and wanted to show off in front of
Lucien. "You don't exactly go out on a limb, do you?" he said.
But he found out to whom he was talking. "You're a little show-
off," Lucien answered, "maybe you think I don't know what you
were doing in the bathroom yesterday? You were puking, old
man!" Berliac grew livid. "Bergère told you?" "Who do you
think?" "All right," Berliac stammered, "but I wouldn't have
thought Bergère would screw his old friends with new ones."
Lucien was a little worried. He had promised Bergère not to repeat anything. "All right, all right," he said, "he didn't screw
you, he just wanted to show me it didn't work." But Berliac turned
his back and left without shaking hands. Lucien was not too
glad when he met Bergère. "What did you say to Berliac?" Bergère asked him neutrally. Lucien lowered his head without answering: he felt overwhelmed. But suddenly he felt Bergère's
hand on his neck: "It doesn't make any difference. In any case,
it had to end: comedians don't amuse me very long." Lucien took
heart; he raised his head and smiled: "But I'm a comedian, too,"
he said, blinking his eyes. "Yes, but you're pretty," Bergère answered, drawing him close. Lucien let himself go; he felt soft as
a girl and tears were in his eyes. Bergère kissed his cheeks and
bit his ear sometimes calling him "my lovely little scoundrel" and
sometimes "my little brother," and Lucien thought it was quite
pleasant to have a big brother who was so indulgent and understanding.

M. and Mme. Fleurier wanted to meet this Bergère of whom
Lucien spoke so much and they invited him to dinner. Everyone
found him charming, including Germaine who had never seen
such a handsome man; M. Fleurier had known General Nizan
who was Bergère's uncle and he spoke of him at great length.
Also, Mme. Fleurier was only too glad to confide Lucien to Bergère for the spring vacation. They went to Rouen by car; Lucien
wanted to see the cathedral and the hôtel-de-ville, but Bergère
flatly refused. "That rubbish?" he asked insolently. Finally, they
spent two hours in a brothel on Rue des Cordeliers and Bergère
was a scream: he called all the chippies "mademoiselle," nudging
Lucien under the table, then he agreed to go up with one of them
but came back after five minutes: "Get the hell out," he gasped,
"it's going to be rough." They paid quickly and left. In the street
Bergère told what happened; while the woman had her back

turned he threw a handful of itching powder on the bed, then told her he was impotent and came down again. Lucien had drunk two whiskeys and was a little tight; he sang the *Artilleur de Metz* and *De Profondis Morpionibus*; he thought it wonderful that Bergère was at the same time so profound and so childish.

"I only reserved one room," Bergère said when they arrived at the hotel, "but there's a big bathroom." Lucien was not surprised: he had vaguely thought during the trip that he would share the room with Bergère without dwelling too much on the idea. Now that he could no longer retreat he found the thing a little disagreeable, especially because his feet were not clean. As the bags were being brought up, he imagined that Bergère would tell him, "How dirty you are, you'll make the sheets black." And he would answer insolently, "Your ideas of cleanliness are really bourgeois." But Bergère shoved him into the bathroom with his bag, saying, "Get yourself ready in there, I'm going to undress in the room." Lucien took a footbath and a sitz bath. He wanted to go to the toilet but he did not dare and contented himself with urinating in the washbasin; then he put on his nightshirt and the slippers his mother lent him (his own were full of holes) and knocked. "Are you ready?" he asked. "Yes, yes, come in." Bergère had slipped a black dressing gown over sky blue pajamas. The room smelled of eau-de-cologne. "Only one bed?" Lucien asked. Bergère did not answer: he looked at Lucien with a stupor that ended in a great burst of laughter. "Look at that shirt!" he said, laughing, "what did you do with your nightcap? Oh no, that's really too funny. I wish you could see yourself." "For two years," Lucien said, angrily, "I've been asking my mother to buy me pajamas." Bergère came toward him. "That's all right. Take it off," he said in a voice to which there was no answer, "I'll give you one of mine. It'll be a little big but it'll be better than that." Lucien stayed rooted in the middle of the room, his eyes riveted on the red and green lozenges of the wallpaper. He would have preferred to go back into the bathroom but he was afraid to act like a fool and with a brisk motion tossed the shirt over his head. There was a moment of silence: Bergère looked at Lucien, smiling, and Lucien suddenly realized he was naked in the middle of the room wearing his mother's pom-pommed slippers. He looked at his hands—the big hands of Rimbaud—he wanted to clutch them to his stomach and cover that at least, but he pulled himself together and put them bravely behind his back. On the walls, between two rows of lozenges, there was a small violet square going back further and further. "My word," said Bergère, "he's as chaste as a virgin: look at yourself in the mirror, Lucien, "you're blushing as far as your chest. But you're still better like that than in a nightshirt." "Yes," Lucien said with effort, "but you never look good when you're naked. Quick, give me the pajamas." Bergère threw him silk pajamas that smelled of lavender and they went to the bed. There was a heavy silence: "I'm sick," Lucien said, "I want to puke." Bergère did not answer and Lucien smelled whiskey in his throat. "He's going to sleep with me," he thought. And the lozenges on the wallpaper began to spin while the stifling smell of eau-de-cologne gagged him. "I shouldn't have said I'd take the trip." He had no luck; twenty times, these last few days, he had almost discovered what Bergère wanted of him and each time, as if on purpose, something happened to turn away his thought. And now he was there, in this man's bed, waiting his good pleasure. I'll take my pillow and go and sleep in the bathroom. But he did not dare; he thought of Bergère's ironic look. He began to laugh, "I'm thinking about the whore a while ago," he said, "she must be scratching now." Bergère still not answer him; Lucien looked at him out of the corner of his eye: he was stretched out innocently on his back, his hands under his head. Then a violent fury seized Lucien, he raised himself on one elbow and asked him, "Well, what are you waiting for? You didn't bring me here to string beads!"

It was too late to regret his words: Bergère turned to him and studied him with an amused eye. "Look at that angel-faced little tart. Well, baby, I didn't make you say it: I'm the one you're counting on to disorder your little senses." He looked at him an instant longer, their faces almost touching, then he took Lucien in his arms and caressed his breast beneath the pajama shirt. It was not unpleasant, it tickled a little, only Bergère was frightening: He looked foolish and repeated with effort, "You aren't ashamed, little pig, you aren't ashamed, little pig!" like the phonograph records in a train station announcing the arrivals and departures. On the contrary, Bergère's hand was swift and light and seemed to be an entire person. It gently grazed Lucien's breast as a caress of warm water in a bath. Lucien wanted to catch this hand, tear it from him and twist it, but Bergère would have laughed: look at that virgin. The hand slid slowly along his belly, stopped a moment to untie the knot of the drawstring which held the trousers. He let him continue: he was heavy and soft as a wet sponge and he was terribly afraid. Bergère had thrown back the

115

covers and put his head on Lucien's breast as though he were listening for a heartbeat. Lucien belched twice in a row and he was afraid of vomiting on the handsome, silver hair so full of dignity. "You're leaning on my stomach," he said. Bergère raised himself a little and passed his hand under Lucien's back; the other hand caressed no longer, it teased. "You have beautiful little buttocks," Bergère said suddenly. Lucien thought he was having a nightmare. "Do you like them?" he said cutely. But Bergère suddenly let him go and raised his head with a spiteful look. "Damned little bluffer," he said angrily, "wants to play Rimbaud and I've been playing with him for an hour and can't even excite him." Tears of rage came to Lucien's eyes and he pushed Bergère away with all his might. "It isn't my fault," he hissed, "you made me drink too much, I want to puke." "All right, go! Go!" Bergère said, "and take your time." Between his teeth he added, "Charming evening." Lucien pulled up his trousers, slipped on the black dressing gown and left. When he had closed the bathroom door he felt so alone and abandoned that he burst out sobbing. There were no handkerchiefs in the pocket of the dressing gown so he wiped his eyes and nose with toilet paper. In vain he pushed his fingers down his throat, he could not vomit. Then he dropped his trousers mechanically and sat down on the toilet, shivering. "The bastard," he thought, "the bastard." He was atrociously humiliated but he did not know whether he was ashamed for having submitted to Bergère's caresses or for not getting excited. The corridor on the other side of the door cracked and Lucien started at each sound but could not decide to go back into the room. "I have to go back," he thought, "I must, or else he'll laugh at me—with Berliac!" and he rose halfway, but as soon as he pictured the face of Bergère and his stupid look, and heard him saying, "You aren't ashamed, little pig?" he fell back on the seat in despair. After a while he was seized with violent diarrhea which soothed him a little: "It's going out by the back," he thought, "I like that better." In fact, he had no further desire to vomit. "He's going to hurt me," he thought suddenly and thought he was going to faint. Finally, he got so cold his teeth began to chatter: he thought he was going to be sick and stood up brusquely. Bergère watched him constrainedly when he went back; he was smoking a cigarette and his pajamas were open and showed his thin torso. Lucien slowly removed his slippers and dressing gown and slipped under the covers without a word. "All right?" asked Bergère. Lucien shrugged. "I'm cold." "Want me to warm you up?" "You can try," Lucien said. At that instant he felt himself crushed by an enormous weight. A warm, soft mouth, like a piece of raw beefsteak, was thrust against his own. Lucien understood nothing more, he no longer knew where he was and he was half smothering, but he was glad because he was warm. He thought of Mme. Besse who pressed her hand against his stomach and called him "my little doll" and Hebrard who called him "big beanpole" and the baths he took in the morning imagining that M. Bouffardier was going to come in and give him an enema and he told himself, "I'm his little doll!" Then Bergère shouted in triumph. "At last!" he said, "you've decided. All right," he added, breathing heavily, "we'll make something out of you." Lucien slipped out of his pajamas.

The next day they awoke at noon. The bellboy brought them breakfast in bed and Lucien thought he looked haughty. "He thinks I'm a fairy," he thought with a shudder of discomfort. Bergère was very nice, he dressed first and went and smoked a cigarette in the old market place while Lucien took his bath. "The thing is," he thought, rubbing himself carefully with a stiff brush, "that it's boring." Once the first moment of terror had passed and he realized that it did not hurt as much as he expected, he had sunk into dismal boredom. He kept hoping it would be over and he could sleep but Bergère had not left him a moment's peace before 4 in the morning. "I've got to finish my trig problem, anyhow," he told himself. And he forced himself not to think of his work any more. The day was long. Bergère told him about the life of Lautréamont, but Lucien did not pay much attention; Bergère annoyed him a little. That night they slept in Caudebec and naturally Bergère disturbed him for a good while, but, around one in the morning, Lucien told him sharply that he was sleepy and Bergère, without getting angry, let him be. They returned to Paris towards the end of the afternoon. All in all, Lucien was not displeased with himself.

His parents welcomed him with open arms: "I hope you at least said thank you to M. Bergère?" his mother asked. He stayed a while to chat with them about the Normandie countryside and went to bed early. He slept like an angel, but on awakening the next day he seemed to be shivering inside. He got up and studied his face for a long time in the mirror. "I'm a pederast," he told himself. And his spirits sank. "Get up, Lucien," his mother called through the door, "you go to school this morning." "Yes, mama," he answered docilely, but let himself drop back onto the bed and began to stare at his toes. "It isn't right, I didn't realize, I have no experience." A man had sucked those toes one after the other. Lucien violently turned his face away: "He knew. What he made me do has a name. It's called sleeping with a man and he knew it." It was funny—Lucien smiled bitterly—for whole days you could ask yourself: am I intelligent, am I stuck-up and you can never decide. And on top of that there were labels which got stuck on to you one fine morning and you had to carry them for the rest of your life: for instance, Lucien was tall and blond, he looked like his father, he was the only son and, since yesterday, he was a pederast. They'd say about him: "Fleurier, you know, the tall blond who loves men?" And people would answer, "Oh yes, the big fairy? Sure, I know who he is."

He dressed and went out but he did not have the heart to go to the lycée. He went down Avenue Lamballe as far as the Seine and followed the quais. The sky was pure, the streets smelled of green leaves, tar and English tobacco. A dreamed-of time to wear clean clothes on a well-washed body and new soul. The people had a moral look; Lucien alone felt suspicious and unusual in this springtime. "The fatal bent," he thought, "I started with an Oedipus complex, after that I became sadico-anal and now the payoff, I'm a pederast; where am I going to stop?" Evidently, his case was not yet very grave: he did not derive much pleasure from Bergère's caresses. "But suppose I get in the habit?" he thought with anguish. "I could never do without it, it'll be like morphine!" He would become a tarnished man, no one would have anything to do with him, his father's workers would laugh when he gave them orders. Lucien imagined his frightful destiny with complacency. He saw himself at 35, gaunt, painted, and already an old gentleman with a moustache and the Legion d'Honneur raising his cane with a terrible look: "Your presence here, sir, is an insult to my daughters." Then suddenly he hesitated and stopped playing: he had just remembered a phrase of Bergère's. At Caudebec during the night, Bergère had said, "So, tell me—are you beginning to get a taste for it?" What did he mean? Naturally, Lucien was not made of wood and after so much caressing . . . "But that doesn't prove anything," he said, worried. But they said that men like that were amazing when it came to spotting other people like them, almost a sixth sense. For a long while Lucien watched a policeman directing traffic at the *Pont d'Iéna*. "Could that policeman excite me?" He stared at the blue trousers of the agent and imagined muscular, hairy thighs.

"Does that do anything to me?" He left, very much comforted. "It's not too bad," he thought, "I can still escape. He took advantage of my disorder but I'm not *really* a pederast." He tried the experiment with every man who crossed his path and each time the result was negative. "Ouf!" he thought, "it was close!" It was a warning, nothing more. He must never start again because a bad habit is taken quickly and then he must absolutely cure himself of these complexes. He resolved to have himself psychoanalyzed by a specialist without telling his parents. Then he would find a mistress and become a man like the others.

Lucien was beginning to reassure himself when suddenly he thought of Bergère: even now, at this very moment Bergère was existing somewhere in Paris, delighted with himself and his head full of memories. "He knows how I'm made, he knows my mouth, he said: you have an odor I shall not forget; he'll go and brag to his friends and say 'I had him' as if I were a girl. Maybe even now he's telling about his nights to—Lucien's heart stopped beating—to Berliac! If he does that I'll kill him: Berliac hates me, he'll tell the whole class, and I'll be sunk, they won't even shake my hand. I'll say it isn't true." Lucien told himself wildly, I'll bring charges, I'll say he raped me!" Lucien hated Bergère with all his strength: without him, without this scandalous irremediable conscience, everything would have been all right, no one would have known and even Lucien himself would eventually have forgotten it. "If he would die suddenly! Dear God, I pray you make him die tonight without telling anybody. Dear God let this whole business be buried, you don't want me to be a pederast. But he's got me!" Lucien thought with rage. "I'll have to go back to him and do whatever he wants and tell him I like it or else I'm lost!" He took a few more steps, then added, as a measure of precaution, "Dear God, make Berliac die, too."

Lucien could not take it upon himself to return to Bergère's house. During the weeks that followed, he thought he met him at every step and, when he was working in his room, he jumped at the sound of a bell; at night he had fearful nightmares: Bergère was raping him in the middle of the Lycée Saint-Louis schoolyard, all the *pistons* were there watching and laughing. But Bergère made no attempt to see him again and gave no sign of life. "He only wanted my body," Lucien thought vexedly. Berliac had disappeared as well and Guigard, who sometimes went to the races with him on Sundays, told Lucien he had left Paris after a nervous breakdown. Lucien grew a little calmer: his trip to Rouen affected him as an obscure, grotesque dream attached to nothing; he had almost forgotten the details, he kept only the impression of a dismal odor of flesh and eau-de-cologne and an intolerable weariness. M. Fleurier sometimes asked what had happened to his friend Bergère: "We'll have to invite him to Férolles to thank him." "He went to New York," Lucien finally answered. Sometimes he went boating on the Marne with Guigard and Guigard's sister taught him to dance. "I'm waking up," he thought, "I'm being reborn." But he still often felt something weighing on his back like a heavy burden: his complexes: he wondered if he should go to Vienna and see Freud: "I'll leave without any money, on foot if I have to, I'll tell him I haven't a cent but I'm a case." One hot afternoon in June, he met The Baboon, his old philosophy prof, on the Boulevard Saint-Michel. "Well, Fleurier," The Baboon said, "you're preparing for Centrale?" "Yes sir," Lucien said. "You should be able," The Baboon said, "to orient yourself toward a study of literature. You were good in philosophy—" "I haven't given it up," Lucien said, "I've done a lot of reading this year, Freud, for instance. By the way," he added, inspired, "I'd like to ask you, Monsieur, what do you think about psychoanalysis?" The Baboon began to laugh: "A fad," he said, "which will pass. The best part of Freud you will find already in Plato. For the rest," he added, in a voice that brooked no answer, "I'll tell you I don't have anything to do with that nonsense. You'd be better off reading Spinoza." Lucien felt himself delivered of an enormous weight and he returned home on foot, whistling. "It was a nightmare," he thought, "nothing more is left of it." The sun was hard and hot that day, but Lucien raised his eyes and gazed at it without blinking: it was the sun of the whole world and Lucien had the right to look it in the face; he was saved! "Nonsense," he thought, "it was nonsense! They tried to drive me crazy but they didn't get me." In fact he had never stopped resisting: Bergère had tripped him up in his reasoning, but Lucien had sensed, for instance, that the pederasty of Rimbaud was a stain, and when that little shrimp Berliac wanted to make him smoke hasheesh Lucien had dressed him down properly: "I risked losing myself," he thought, "but what protected me was my moral health!" That evening, at dinner, he looked at his father with sympathy. M. Fleurier had square shoulders and the slow heavy gestures of a peasant with something racial in them and his grey boss's eyes, metallic and cold. "I look like him," Lucien thought. He remembered that the Fleuriers, father and son, had been captains of industry for four generations: "Say what you want, the family exists!" And he thought proudly of the moral health of the Fleuriers.

Lucien did not present himself for the examinations at the Ecole Centrale that year and the Fleuriers left very shortly for Férolles. He was charmed to find the house again, the garden, the factory, the calm and poised little town. It was another world: he decided to get up early in the mornings and take long walks through the country. "I want," he told his father, "to fill my lungs with pure air and store up health for next year." He accompanied his mother to the Bouffardiers and the Besses and everyone thought he had become a big, well-poised and reasonable boy. Hebrard and Winckelmann, who were taking law courses in Paris, had come back to Férolles for a vacation. Lucien went out with them several times and they talked about the jokes they used to play on Abbé Jacquemart, their long bicycle trips and they sang the *Artilleur de Metz* in harmony. Lucien keenly appreciated the rough frankness and solidity of his old friends and he reproached himself for having neglected them. He confessed to Hebrard that he did not care much for Paris, but Hebrard could not understand it: his parents had entrusted him to an abbé and he was very much held in check; he was still dazzled by his visits to the Louvre and the evening he had spent at the Opera. Lucien was touched by his simplicity; he felt himself the elder brother of Hebrard and Winckelmann and he began to tell himself he did not regret having had such a tormented life: he had gained experience. He told them about Freud and psychoanalysis and amused himself by shocking them a little. They violently criticized the theory of complexes but their objections were naive and Lucien pointed it out to them, then he added that from a philosophical viewpoint it was easy to refute the errors of Freud. They admired him greatly but Lucien pretended not to notice it.

M. Fleurier explained the operation of the factory to Lucien. He took him on a visit through the central buildings and Lucien watched the workers at great length. "If I should die," M. Fleurier said, "you'd have to take command of the factory at a moment's notice." Lucien scolded him and said, "Don't talk like that, will you please, papa." But he was serious for several days in a row thinking of the responsibilities which would fall on him sooner or later. They had long talks about the duties of the boss and M. Fleurier showed him that ownership was not a right but a duty: "What are they trying to give us, with their class struggle," he said, "as though the interests of the bosses and the workers were just the opposite. Take my case, Lucien, I'm a little boss, what they call small fry. Well, I make a living for 100 workers and their families. If I do well, they're the first ones to profit. But if I have to close the plant, there they are in the street. *I don't have a right*," he said forcefully, "to do bad business. And that's what I call the solidarity of classes."

All went well for more than three weeks; he almost never thought of Bergère; he had forgiven him: he simply hoped never to see him again for the rest of his life. Sometimes, when he changed his shirt, he went to the mirror and looked at himself with astonishment: "A man has desired this body," he thought. He passed his hands slowly over his legs and thought: "A man was excited by these legs." He touched his back and regretted not being another person to be able to caress his own flesh like a piece of silk. Sometimes he missed his complexes: they had been solid, heavy, their enormous somber mass had balanced him. Now it was finished, Lucien no longer believed in it and he felt terribly unstable. Though it was not so unpleasant, it was rather a sort of very tolerable disenchantment, a little upsetting, which could, if necessary, pass for *ennui*. "I'm nothing," he thought, "but it's because nothing has soiled me. Berliac was soiled and caught. I can stand a little uncertainty: it's the price of purity."

During a walk, he sat down on a hillock and thought: "For six years I slept, and then one fine day I came out of my cocoon." He was animated and looked affably around the countryside. "I'm built for action," he thought. But in an instant his thought of glory faded. He whispered, "Let them wait a while and they'll see what I'm worth." He had spoken with force but the words rolled on his lips like empty shells. "What's the matter with me?" He did not want to recognize this odd inquietude, it had hurt him too much before. He thought, "It's this silence . . . this land. . . ." Not a living being, save crickets laboriously dragging their black and yellow bellies in the dust. Lucien hated crickets because they always looked half dead. On the other side of the road, a greyish stretch of land, crushed, creviced, ran as far as the river. No one saw Lucien, no one heard him; he sprang to his feet and felt that his movements would meet with no resistance, not even that of gravity. Now he stood beneath a curtain of grey clouds; it was as though he existed in a vacuum. "This silence . . ." he thought. It was more than silence, it was nothingness. The countryside was extraordinarily calm and soft about Lucien, inhuman: it seemed that it was making itself tiny and was holding its breath so as not to disturb him. "*Quand l'artilleur de Metz revint en garnison. . . .*" The sound died on his lips as a flame in a vacuum: Lucien was alone, without a shadow and without echo, in the midst of this too discreet nature which meant nothing. He shook himself and tried to recapture the thread of his thought. "I'm built for action. First, I can bounce back: I can do a lot of foolishness but it doesn't go far because I always spring back." He thought, "I have moral health." But he stopped, making a grimace of disgust, it seemed so absurd to him to speak of "moral health" on this white road crossed by dying insects. In rage, Lucien stepped on a cricket, under his sole he felt a little elastic ball and, when he raised his foot, the cricket was still alive: Lucien spat on it. "I'm perplexed, I'm perplexed. It's like last year." He began to think about Winckelmann who called him "the ace of aces," about M. Fleurier who treated him like a man, Mme. Besse who told him, "This is the big boy I used to call my little doll, I wouldn't dare say it now, he frightens me." But they were far, far away and it seemed the real Lucien was lost, that there was only a white and perplexed larva. "What am I?" Miles and miles of land, a flat, chapped soil, grassless, odorless, and then, suddenly springing straight from this grey crust, the beanpole, so unwonted that there was even no shadow behind it. "What am I?" The question had not changed since the past vacation, it was as if it waited for Lucien at the very spot he had left it; or, it wasn't a question, but a condition. Lucien shrugged his shoulders. "I'm too scrupulous," he thought, "I analyze myself too much."

The following days he forced himself to stop analyzing: he wanted to let himself be fascinated by things, lengthily he studied egg cups, napkin rings, trees, and store fronts; he flattered his mother very much when he asked her if she would like to show him her silver service; he thought he was looking at silver and behind the look throbbed a little living fog. In vain Lucien absorbed himself in conversation with M. Fleurier, this abundant, tenacious mist, whose opaque inconsistency falsely resembled light, slipped *behind* the attention he gave his father's words: this fog was himself. From time to time, annoyed, Lucien stopped listening, turned away, tried to catch the fog and look it in the face: he found only emptiness, the fog was still *behind*.

Germaine came in tears to Mme. Fleurier: her brother had

broncho-pneumonia. "My poor Germaine," Mme. Fleurier said, "and you always said how strong he was!" She gave her a month's vacation and, to replace her, brought in the daughter of one of the factory workers, little Berthe Mozelle who was seventeen. She was small, with blond plaits rolled about her head; she limped slightly. Since she came from Concarneau, Mme. Fleurier begged her to wear a lace coiffe, "That would be so much nicer." From the first days, each time she met Lucien, her wide blue eyes reflected a humble and passionate adoration and Lucien realized she worshipped him. He spoke to her familiarly and often asked her "Do you like it here?" In the hallways he amused himself making passes at her to see if they had an effect. But she touched him deeply and he drew a precious comfort from this love; he often thought with a sting of emotion of the image Berthe must make of him. "By the simple fact that I hardly look like the young workers she goes out with." On a pretext he took Winckelmann into the pantry and Winckelmann thought she was well built: "You're a lucky dog," he concluded, "I'd look into it if I were you." But Lucien hesitated: she smelled of sweat and her black blouse was eaten away under the arms. One rainy day in September M. Fleurier drove into Paris and Lucien stayed in his room alone. He lay down on his bed and began to yawn. He seemed to be a cloud, capricious and fleeting, always the same, always something else, always diluting himself in the air. "I wonder why I exist?" He was there, he digested, he yawned, he heard the rain tapping on the windowpanes and the white fog was unravelling in his head: and then? His existence was a scandal and the responsibilities he would assume later would barely be enough to justify it. "After all, I didn't ask to be born," he said. And he pitied himself. He remembered his childhood anxieties, his long somnolences and they appeared to him in a new light: fundamentally, he had not stopped being embarrassed with his life, with this voluminous, useless gift, and he had carried it in his arms without knowing what to do with it or where to set it down. "I have spent my time regretting I was born." But he was too depressed to push his thoughts further; he rose, lit a cigarette and went down into the kitchen to ask Berthe to make some tea.

She did not see him enter. He touched her shoulder and she started violently. "Did I frighten you?" he asked. She looked at him fearfully, leaning both hands on the table and her breast heaved: after a moment she smiled and said, "It scared me, I didn't think anybody was there." Lucien returned her smile with indulgence and said, "It would be very nice if you'd make a little tea for me." "Right away, Monsieur Lucien," the girl answered and she went to the stove: Lucien's presence seemed to make her uncomfortable. Lucien remained on the doorstep, uncertain. "Well," he asked paternally, "do you like it here with us?" Berthe turned her back on him and filled a pan at the spigot. The sound of the water covered her answer. Lucien waited a moment and when she had set the pan on the gas range he continued, "Have you ever smoked?" "Sometimes," the girl answered, warily. He opened his pack of cigarettes and held it out to her. He was not too pleased: he felt he was compromising himself; he shouldn't make her smoke. "You want . . . me to smoke?" she asked, surprised. "Why not?" "Madame will scold me." Lucien had an unpleasant impression of complicity. He began to laugh and said, "We won't tell her." Berthe blushed, took a cigarette with the tips of her fingers and put it in her mouth. Should I offer to light it? That wouldn't be right. He said to her, "Well, aren't you going to light it?" She annoyed him; she stood there, her arms stiff, red and docile, her lips bunched around the cigarette like a thermometer stuck in her mouth. She finally took a sulphur match from the tin box, struck it, smoked a few puffs with her eyes half shut and said, "It's mild." Then she hurriedly took the cigarette from her mouth and clutched it awkwardly between her five fingers. "A born victim," Lucien thought. Yet, she thawed a little when he asked her if she liked her Brittany, she described the different sorts of Breton coiffes to him and even sang a song from Rosporden in a soft, off-key voice. Lucien teased her gently but she did not understand the joke and looked at him fearfully: at those times she looked like a rabbit. He was sitting on a stool and felt quite at ease: "Sit down," he told her. . . . "Oh no, Monsieur Lucien, not before Monseiur Lucien." He took her under the arms and drew her to his knees. "And like that?" he asked. She let herself go, murmuring, "On your knees!" with an air of ecstasy and reproach with a funny accent and Lucien thought wearily, "I'm getting too much involved, I shouldn't have gone so far." He was silent: she stayed on his knees, hot, quiet, but Lucien felt her heart beating. "She belongs to me," he thought, "I can do anything I want with her." He let her go, took the teapot and went back to his room: Berthe did not make a move to stop him. Before drinking his tea, Lucien washed his hands with his mother's scented soap because they smelled of armpits.

"Am I going to sleep with her?" In the following days Lucien was absorbed in this small problem; Berthe was always putting herself in his way, looking at him with the great sad eyes of a spaniel. Morality won out: Lucien realized he risked making her pregnant because he did not have enough experience (impossible to buy contraceptives in Férolles, he was too well known) and he would cause M. Fleurier much worry. He also told himself that later he would have less authority in the factory if one of the worker's daughters could brag he had slept with her. "I don't have the right to touch her." He avoided being alone with Berthe during the last days of September. "So," Winckelmann asked him, "What are you waiting for?" "I'm not going to bother," Lucien answered dryly, "I don't like ancillary love." Winckelmann, who heard the words "ancillary love" for the first time, gave a low whistle and was silent.

Lucien was very satisfied with himself; he had conducted himself like a *chic type* and that repaid many errors. "She was ripe for it," he told himself with a little regret, but on reconsidering it, he thought, "It's the same as though I had her: she offered herself and I didn't want her." And henceforth he no longer considered himself a virgin. These slight satisfactions occupied his mind for several days. Then they, too, melted into the fog. Returning to school in October, he felt as dismal as at the beginning of the previous year.

Berliac had not come back and no one had heard anything about him. Lucien noticed several unknown faces. His right-hand neighbor whose name was Lemordant had taken a year of special mathematics in Poitiers. He was even bigger than Lucien, and with his black moustache, already looked like a man. Lucien met his friends again without pleasure: they seemed childish to him and innocently boisterous: schoolboys. He still associated himself with their collective manifestations but with nonchalance, as was permitted him by his position of *carré*. Lemordant would have attracted him more, because he was mature; but, unlike Lucien, he did not seem to have acquired that maturity through multiple and painful experiences: he was an adult by birth. Lucien often contemplated with a full satisfaction that voluminous, pensive head, neckless, planted awry on the shoulders: it seemed impossible to get anything into it, neither through the ears, nor the tiny slanting eyes, pink and glassy: "man with convictions," Lucien thought with respect; and he wondered, not without jealousy, what that certitude could be that gave Lemordant such a full consciousness of self. "That's how I should be; a rock." He was even a little surprised that Lemordant should be accessible to mathematical reasoning; but M. Husson convinced him when he gave back the first papers: Lucien was seventh and Lemordant had been given a "5" and 78th place; all was in order. Lemordant gave no sign; he seemed to expect the worst. His tiny mouth, his heavy cheeks, yellow and smooth, were not made to express feelings: he was a Buddha. They saw him angry only once, the day Loewy bumped into him in the cloakroom. First, he gave a dozen sharp little growls, and blinked his eyes: "Back to Poland," he said at last, "to Poland you dirty kike and don't come crapping around here with us." He dominated Loewy with his whole form and his massive chest swayed on his long legs. He finished up by slapping him and little Loewy apologized: the affair ended there.

On Thursdays, Lucien went out with Guigard who took him dancing with his sister's girl friends. But Guigard finally confessed that these hops bored him. "I've got a girl," he confided, "a *première* in Plisnier's, Rue Royale. She has a friend who doesn't have anybody: you ought to come with us Saturday night." Lucien made a scene with his parents and got permission to go out every Saturday; they left the key under the mat for him. He met Guigard around nine o'clock in a bar on the Rue Saint-Honoré. "You wait and see," Guigard said, "Fanny is charming and what's nice about her is she really knows how to dress." "what about mine?" "I don't know her; I know she's an apprentice dressmaker and she's just come to Paris from Angoûlème. By the way," he added, "don't pull any boners. My name's Pierre Daurat. You, because you're blond, I said you were part English, it's better. Your name's Lucien Bonnières." "But why?" asked Lucien, intrigued. "My boy," Guigard answered, "it's a rule. You can do what you like with these girls but never tell your name." "All right," Lucien said, "what do I do for a living?" "You can say you're a student, that's better, you understand, it flatters them and then you don't have to spend much money. Of course, we share the expenses; but let me pay this evening; I'm in the habit: I'll tell you what you owe me on Monday." Immediately Lucien thought Guigard was trying to get a rake-off. "God, how distrustful I've gotten!" he thought with amusement. Just then Fanny came in: a tall, thin brunette with long thighs and a heavily rouged face. Lucien found her intimidating. "Here's Bonnières I was telling you about," Guigard said. "Pleased to meet you,"

Fanny said with a myopic look. "This is my girl friend Maud." Lucien saw an ageless little woman wearing a hat that looked like an overturned flower pot. She was not rouged and appeared greyish after the dazzling Fanny. Lucien was bitterly disappointed but he saw she had a pretty mouth—and then there was no need to be embarrassed with her. Guigard had taken care to pay for the beers in advance so that he could profit from the commotion of their arrival to push the two girls gaily toward the door without allowing them the time for a drink. Lucien was grateful to him: M. Fleurier only gave him 125 francs a week and out of this money he had to pay carfare. The evening was amusing; they went dancing in the Latin Quarter in a hot, pink little place with dark corners and where a cocktail cost five francs. There were many students with girls of the same type as Fanny but not as good looking. Fanny was superb: she looked straight in the eyes of a big man with a beard who smoked a pipe and said very loudly, "I hate people who smoke pipes at dances." The man turned crimson and put the lighted pipe back in his pocket. She treated Guigard and Lucien with a certain condescension and sometimes told them, "You're a couple of kids," with a gentle, maternal air. Lucien felt full of ease and sweetness; he told Fanny several amusing little things and smiled while telling them. Finally, the smile never left his face and he was able to hit on a refined tone of voice with touches of devil-may-care and tender courtesy tinged with irony. But Fanny spoke little to him; she took Guigard's chin and pulled his cheeks to make his mouth stand out; when the lips were full and drooling a little, like fruit swollen with juice or like snails, she licked them, saying, "Baby." Lucien was horribly annoyed and thought Guigard was ridiculous: Guigard had rouge near his lips and fingermarks on his cheeks. But the behavior of the other couples was even more negligent: everyone kissed; from time to time the girl from the checkroom passed among them with a little basket, throwing streamers and multicolored balls shouting, "Olè, les enfants, amusez-vous, Olè, olè!" and everybody laughed. At last Lucien remembered the existence of Maud and he said to her, smiling, "Look at those turtle doves. . . ." He pointed to Fanny and Guigard and added, "nous autres, nobles vieillards. . . ." He did not finish the phrase but smiled so drolly that Maud smiled too. She removed her hat and Lucien saw with pleasure that she was somewhat better than the other women in the dance hall; then he asked her to dance and told her the jokes he played on his professors the year of his baccalaureat. She danced well, her eyes were black and serious and she had an intelligent look. Lucien told her about Berthe and said he was full of remorse. "But," he added, "it was better for her." Maud thought the story about Berthe was poetic and sad, she asked how much Berthe earned from Lucien's parents. "It's not always funny," she added, "for a young girl to be in the family way." Guigard and Fanny paid no more attention to them, they caressed each other and Guigard's face was covered with moisture. From time to time Lucien repeated, "Look at those turtle doves, just look at them!" and he had his sentence ready, "They make me feel like doing it too." But he dared not say it and contented himself with smiling, then he pretended that he and Maud were old friends, disdainful of love and he called her "brother" and made as if to slap her on the back. Suddenly, Fanny turned her head and looked at them with surprise, "Well," she said, "first-graders, how're you doing? Why don't you kiss, you're dying to." Lucien took Maud in his arms; he was a little annoyed because Fanny was watching them: he wanted the kiss to be long and successful but he wondered how people breathed. Finally, it was not as difficult as he thought, it was enough to kiss on an angle, leaving the nostrils clear. He heard Guigard counting "one—two—three—four—" and he let go of Maud at 52. "Not bad for a beginning," Guigard said. "I can do better." Lucien looked at his wrist watch and counted: Guigard left Fanny's mouth at the 159th second. Lucien was furious and thought the contest was stupid. "I let go of Maud just to be safe," he thought, "but that's nothing, once you know how to breathe you can keep on forever." He proposed a second match and won. When it was all over, Maud looked at Lucien and said seriously, "You kiss well." Lucien blushed with pleasure. "At your service," he answered, bowing. Still he would rather have kissed Fanny. They parted around half past twelve because of the last metro. Lucien was joyful; he leaped and danced in the Rue Raynouard and thought, "It's in the bag." The corners of his mouth hurt because he had smiled so much.

He saw Maud every Thursday at six and on Saturday evening. She let herself be kissed but nothing more. Lucien complained to Guigard who reassured him, "Don't worry," Guigard said, "Fanny's sure she'll lay; but she's young and only had two boys; Fanny says for you to be very tender with her." "Tender?" Lucien said. "Get a load of that!" They both laughed and Guigard concluded, "That's what you've got to do." Lucien was very tender. He kissed Maud a lot and told her he loved her, but after a while it became a little monotonous and then he was not too proud of going out with her: he would have liked to give her advice on how she should dress, but she was full of prejudices and angered quickly. Between kisses, they were silent, gazing at each other and holding hands. "God knows what she's thinking with those strict eyes she has." Lucien still thought of the same thing: this small existence, sad and vague, which was his own, and told himself, "I wish I were Lemordant, there's a man who's found his place!" During those times he saw himself as though he were another person: sitting near a woman who loved him, his hand in hers, his lips still wet from kisses, refusing the humble happiness she offered him: alone. Then he clasped Maud's fingers tightly and tears came to his eyes: he would have liked to make her happy.

One morning in December, Lemordant came up to Lucien; he held a paper. "You want to sign?" he asked. "What is it?" "Because of the kikes at the Normale Sup; they sent the *Oeuvre* a petition against compulsory military training with 200 signatures. So we're protesting; we need a thousand names at least: we're going to get the *cyrards*, the *flottards*, the *agros*, the X's and the whole works." Lucien was flattered. "Is it going to be printed?" "Surely in *Action*. Maybe in *Echo de Paris* besides." Lucien wanted to sign on the spot but he thought it would not be wise. He took the paper and read it carefully. Lemordant added, "I hear you don't have anything to do with politics; that's your business. But you're French and you've got a right to have your say." When he heard "you've got a right to have your say," Lucien felt an inexplicable and rapid joy. He signed. The next day he bought *Action Française* but the proclamation was not there. It didn't appear until Thursday, Lucien found it on the second page under the headline: YOUTH OF FRANCE SCORES IN TEETH OF INTERNATIONAL JEWRY. His name was there, compressed, definitive, not far from Lemordant's, almost as strange as the names *Fleche* and *Flipot* which surrounded it; it looked unreal. "Lucien Fleurier," he thought, "a peasant name, a real French name." He read the whole series of names starting with F aloud and when it came to his turn he pronounced it as if he did not recognize it. Then he stuffed the newspaper in his pocket and went home happily.

A few days later he sought out Lemordant. "Are you active in politics?" he asked. "I'm in the League," Lemordant said, "Ever read *Action Française?*" "Not much," Lucien confessed. "Up to now it didn't interest me but I think I'm changing my mind." Lemordant looked at him without curiosity, with his impenetrable air. Lucien told him, in a few words, what Bergère had called his "disorder." "Where do you come from?" Lemordant asked. "Férolles. My father has a factory there." "How long did you stay there?" "Till second form." "I see," Lemordant said, "it's very simple, you're uprooted. Have you read Barrès?" "I read *Colette Baudoche.*" "Not that," Lemordant said impatiently, "I'll bring you the *Deracinés* this afternoon. That's your story. You'll find the cause and cure." The book was bound in green leather. On the first page was an *"ex libris* André Lemordant" in gothic letters. Lucien was surprised; he had never dreamed Lemordant could have a first name.

He began reading it with much distrust: it had been explained to him so many times: so many times had he been lent books with a "Read this, it fits you perfectly," Lucien thought with a sad smile that he was not someone who could be set down in so many pages. The Oedipus complex, the disorder: what childishness, and so far away! But, from the very first, he was captivated: in the first place, it was not psychology—Lucien had a bellyful of psychology—the young people Barrès described were not abstract individuals or declassed like Rimbaud or Verlaine, nor sick like the unemployed Viennese who had themselves psychoanalyzed by Freud. Barrès began by placing them in their milieu, in their family: they had been well brought up, in the provinces, in solid traditions. Lucien thought Sturel resembled himself. "It's true," he said, "I'm uprooted." He thought of the moral health of the Fleuriers, a health acquired only in the land, their physical strength (his grandfather used to twist a bronze sou between his fingers); he remembered with emotion the dawns in Férolles: he rose, tiptoed down the stairs so as not to wake his family, straddled his bicycle and the soft countryside of the Ile de France enveloped him in its discreet caresses. "I've always hated Paris," he thought with force. He also read the *Jardin de Bérénice* and, from time to time, stopped reading and began to ponder, his eyes vague; thus they were again offering him a character and a destiny, a means of escaping the inexhaustible gossip of his conscience, a method of defining and appreciating himself. And how much he preferred the unconscious, reeking of the soil, which Barrès gave him, to the filthy, lascivious images of Freud. To grasp it, Lucien had only to turn himself away from a sterile and dangerous contemplation of self: he must study the soil and subsoil of Férolles, he must decipher the sense of the rolling hills which descended as far as the Sernette, he must apply himself to human geography and history. Or, simply return to Férolles and live there: he would find it harmless and fertile at his feet, stretched across the countryside, mixed in the woods, the springs, and the grass like nourishing humus from which Lucien could at last draw the strength to become a leader. Lucien left these long dreams exalted, and sometimes felt as if he had found his road. Now he was silent close to Maud, his arm about her waist, the words, the scraps of sentences resounding in him: "renew tradition," "the earth and the dead"; deep, opaque words, inexhaustible. "How tempting it is," he thought. Yet he dared not believe it: he had already been disappointed too often. He opened up his fears to Lemordant: "It would be too good." "My boy," Lemordant answered, "you don't believe everything you want to right away: you need practice." He thought a little and said, "You ought to come with us." Lucien accepted with an open heart, but he insisted on keeping his liberty, "I'll come," he said, "but I won't be involved. I want to see and think about it."

Lucien was captivated by the camaraderie of the young *camelots*; they gave him a cordial, simple welcome and he immediately felt at ease in their midst. He soon knew Lemordant's "gang," about 20 students almost all of whom wore velvet berets. They held their meetings on the second floor of the Polder beer-hall where they played bridge and billiards. Lucien often went there to meet them and soon he realized they had adopted him for he was always greeted with shouts of *"Voilà le plus beau!"* or "Our National Fleurier!" But it was their good humor which especially captured Lucien: nothing pedantic or austere; little talk of politics. They laughed and sang, that was all, they shouted or beat the tables in honor of the student youth. Lemordant himself smiled without dropping an authority which no one would have dared question. Lucien was more often silent, his look wandering over these boisterous, muscular young people. "This is strength," he thought. Little by little he discovered the true sense of youth in the midst of them: it was not in the affected grace Bergère appreciated; youth was the future of France. However, Lemordant's friends did not have the troubled charm of adolescence: they were adults and several wore beards. Looking closely he found an air of parenthood in all of them: they had finished with the wanderings and uncertainties of their age, they had nothing more to learn, they were made. In the beginning their lighthearted, ferocious jokes somewhat shocked Lucien: one might have thought them without conscience. When Rémy announced that Mme. Dubus, the wife of the radical leader, had her legs cut off by a truck, Lucien expected them to render a brief homage to their unfortunate adversary. But they all burst out laughing and slapped their legs saying: "The old carrion!" and "What a fine truck driver!" Lucien was a little taken back but suddenly he understood that this great, purifying laughter was a refusal: they had scented danger, they wanted no cowardly pity and they were firm. Lucien began to laugh too. Little by little their pranks appeared to him in their true light: there was only the shell of frivolity; at heart it was the affirmation of a right: their conviction was so deep, so religious, that it gave them the right to appear frivolous, to dismiss all that was not essential with a whim, a pirouette. Between the icy humor of Charles Maurras and the jokes of Desperreau, for instance (he carried in his pocket an old condom end which he called Blum's foreskin) there was only a difference of degree. In January the University announced a solemn meeting in the course of which the degree of *doctor honoris causa* was to be bestowed on two Swedish mineralogists. "You're going to see something good," Lemordant told Lucien, giving him an invitation card. The big amphitheatre was packed. When Lucien saw the President of the Republic and the Rector enter at the sound of the *Marseillaise,* his heart began to pound, he was afraid for his friends. Just then a few young people rose from their seats and began to shout. With sympathy Lucien recognized Rémy, red as a beet, struggling between two men who were pulling his coat, shouting, "France for the French!" But he was especially pleased to see an old gentleman, with the air of a precocious child, blowing a little horn. "How healthy it is," he thought. He keenly tasted this odd mixture of headstrong gravity and turbulence which gave the youngest an air of maturity and the oldest an impish air. Soon Lucien himself tried to joke. He had some success and when he said of Herriot, "There's no more God if he dies in his bed," he felt the birth of a sacred fury in him. Then he gritted his teeth and, for a moment, felt as convinced, as strict, as powerful as Rémy or Desperreau. "Lemordant is right," he thought, "you need practice, it's all there." He also learned to avoid discussions: Guigard, who was only a republican, overwhelmed him with objections. Lucien listened to him politely but, after a while, shut up. Guigard was still talking, but

133

Lucien did not even look at him any more: he smoothed the fold in his trousers and amused himself by blowing smoke rings with his cigarette and looking at women. Nevertheless, he heard a few of Guigard's objections, but they quickly lost their weight and slipped off him, light and futile. Guigard finally was quiet, quite impressed. Lucien told his parents about his new friends and M. Fleurier asked him if he was going to be a *camelot*. Lucien hesitated and gravely said, "I'm tempted, I'm really tempted." "Lucien, I beg you, don't do it," his mother said, "they're very excitable and something bad can happen so quickly. Don't you see you can get in trouble or be put in prison? Besides, you're much too young to be mixed up in politics." Lucien answered her only with a firm smile and M. Fleurier intervened, "Let him alone, dear," he said gently, "let him follow his own ideas; he has to pass through it." From that day on it seemed to Lucien that his parents treated him with a certain consideration. Yet he did not decide; these few weeks had taught him much: by turn he considered the benevolent curiosity of his father, Mme. Fleurier's worries, the growing respect of Guigard, the insistence of Lemordant and the impatience of Rémy and, nodding his head, he told himself, "This is no small matter." He had a long conversation with Lemordant and Lemordant well understood his reasons and told him not to hurry. Lucien still was nostalgic: he had the impressions of being only a small gelatinous transparency trembling on the seat in a café and the boisterous agitation of the *camelots* seemed absured to him. But at other times he felt hard and heavy as a rock and he was almost happy.

He got along better and better with the whole gang. He sang them the *Noce à Rebecca* which Hébrard had taught him the previous vacation and everyone thought it was tremendously amusing. Lucien threw out several biting reflections about the Jews and spoke of Berliac who was so miserly: "I always asked myself: why is he so cheap, it isn't possible to be that cheap. Then one day I understood: he was one of the tribe." Everybody began to laugh and a sort of exaltation came over Lucien: he felt truly furious about the Jews and the memory of Berliac was deeply unpleasant to him. Lemordant looked him in the eyes and said, "You're a real one, you are." After that they often asked Lucien: "Fleurier, tell us a good one about the kikes." And Lucien told the Jewish jokes he learned from his father; all he had to do was begin, "Vun day Levy met Bloom . . ." to fill his friends with mirth. One day Rémy and Patenotre told how they had come across an Algerian Jew by the Seine and how they had almost frightened him to death by acting as if they were going to throw him in the water: "I said to myself," Rémy concluded, "what a shame it was Fleurier wasn't with us." "Maybe it was better he wasn't there," Desperreau interrupted, "he'd have chucked him in the water for good!" There was no one like Lucien for recognizing a Jew from the nose. When he went out with Guigard he nudged his elbow: "Don't turn around now: the little short one, behind us, he's one of them!" "For that," Guigard said, "you can really smell 'em out." Fanny could not stand the Jews either; all four of them went to Maud's room one Thursday and Lucien sang the *Noce à Rebecca*. Fanny could stand no more, she said, "Stop, stop, or I'll wet my pants." And when he had finished, she gave him an almost tender look. They played jokes on him in the Polder beerhall. There was always someone to say, negligently, "Fleurier who likes the Jews so much . . ." or "Leon Blum, the great friend of Fleurier . . ." and the others waited, in stitches, holding their breath, open mouthed. Lucien grew red and struck the table, shouting, "God damn . . . !" and they burst out laughing and said, "He bit! He bit! He didn't bite—he swallowed it!"

He often went to political meetings with them and heard Professor Claude and Maxime Real Del Sarte. His work suffered a little from these new obligations, but, since Lucien could not count on winning the Centrale scholarship anyhow, that year, M. Fleurier was indulgent. "After all," he told his wife, "Lucien must learn the job of being a man." After these meetings Lucien and his friends felt hot-headed and were given to playing tricks. Once about ten of them came across a little, olive skinned man who was crossing the Rue Saint-André-des-Arts, reading *Humanité*. They shoved him into a wall and Rémy ordered "Throw down that paper." The little man wanted to act up but Desperreau slipped behind him and grabbed him by the waist while Lemordant ripped the paper from his grasp with a powerful fist. It was very amusing. The little man, furious, kicked the air and shouted "Let go of me! Let go!" with an odd accent and Lemordant, quite calm, tore up the paper. But things were spoiled when Desperreau wanted to let the man go: he threw himself on Lemordant and would have struck him if Rémy hadn't landed a good punch behind his ear just in time. The man fell against the wall and looked at them all evilly, saying *"Sales Français!"* "Say that again," Marchesseau demanded coldly. Lucien realized there was going to be some dirty work: Marchesseau could not take a joke when it was a question of France. "*Sales Français!*" the dago said. He was slapped again and threw himself forward, his head lowered, "*Sales Français, sales bourgeois,* I hate you, I hope you croak, all of you, all of you!" and a flood of other filthy curses with a violence that Lucien never imagined possible. Then they lost patience and all had to step in and give him a good lesson. After a while they let him go and the man dropped against the wall: his breath was a whistle, one punch had closed his left eye and they were all around him, tired of striking him, waiting for him to fall. The man twisted his mouth and spat: "*Sales Francais, sales Français.*" There was a moment of hesitation and Lucien realized his friends were going to give it up. Then it was stronger than he was, he leaped forward and struck with all his might. He heard something crack and the little man looked at him with surprise and weakness. "*Sales . . .*" he muttered, but his puffed eye began to open on a red, sightless globe; he fell to his knees and said nothing more. "Get the hell out," Rémy hissed. They ran, stopping only at Place Saint-Michel: no one was following them. They straightened their ties and brushed each other off.

The evening passed without mention of the incident and the young men were especially nice to each other: they had abandoned the modest brutality which usually veiled their feelings. They spoke politely to each other and Lucien thought that for the first time they were acting as they acted with their families; but he was enervated: he was not used to fighting thugs in the middle of the street. He thought tenderly of Maud and Fanny.

He could not sleep. "I can't go on," he thought, "following them like an amateur. Everything has been weighted, I *must* join!" He felt grave and almost religious when he announced the good news to Lemordant. "It's decided," he said, "I'm with you." Lemordant slapped him on the shoulder and the gang celebrated the event by polishing off several bottles. They had recovered their gay and brutal tone and talked only about the incident of the night before. As they were about to leave, Marchesseau told Lucien simply, "You've got a terrific punch!" and Lucien answered, "He was a Jew."

The day after that he went to see Maud with a heavy malacca cane he had bought in a store on the Boulevard St. Michel. Maud understood immediately: she looked at the cane and said, "So you did it?" "I did it," Lucien smiled. Maud seemed flattered; personally, she favored the ideas of the Left, but she was broad-minded. "I think," she said, "there's good in all parties." In the course of the evening, she scratched his neck several times and called him "My little *camelot*." A little while after that, one Saturday night, Maud felt tired. "I think I'll go back," she said, "but you can come up with me if you're good: you can hold my hand and be real nice to your little Maud who's so tired, and you can tell her stories." Lucien was hardly enthusiastic: Maud's room depressed him with its careful poverty: it was like a maid's room. But it would have been criminal to let such an opportunity pass by. Hardly in the room, Maud threw herself on the bed, saying, "Whew! it feels so good!" Then she was silent, gazing into Lucien's eyes, and puckered her lips. He stretched himself out near her and she put her hand over his eyes, spreading her fingers and saying, "Peekaboo, I see you, you know I see you, Lucien!" He felt soft and heavy, she put her fingers in his mouth and he sucked them, then spoke to her tenderly, "Poor little Maud's sick, does little Maud have a pain?" and he caressed her whole body; she had closed her eyes and was smiling mysteriously. After a moment he raised her skirt and they made love; Lucien thought, "What a break!" When it was over Maud said, "Well, if I'd thought that!" She looked at Lucien with a tender reproach. "Naughty boy, I thought you were going to be good!" Lucien said he was as surprised as she was. "That's the way it happens," he said. She thought a little and then told him seriously, "I don't regret anything. Before maybe it was purer but it wasn't so complete."

In the métro, Lucien thought "I have a mistress." He was empty and tired, saturated with a smell of absinthe and fresh fish; he sat down, holding himself stiffly to avoid contact with his sweat-soaked shirt; he felt his body to be curdled milk. He repeated forcefully, "I have a mistress." But he felt frustrated: what he desired in Maud the night before was her narrow, closed face which seemed so unattainable, her slender silhouette, her look of dignity, her reputation for being a serious girl, her scorn of the masculine sex, all those things that made her a strange being, truly *someone else*, hard and definitive, always out of reach, with her clean little thoughts, her modesties, her silk stockings and crepe dresses, her permanent wave. And all this veneer had melted under his embrace, the flesh remained, he had stretched his lips toward an eyeless face, naked as a belly, he had possessed a great flower of moist flesh. Again he saw the blind beast throbbing in the sheets with rippling, hairy yawns and he thought: that was *us two.* They had made a single one, he could no longer distinguish his flesh from that of Maud; no one had ever given him that feeling of sickening intimacy, except possibly Riri, when Riri showed him his wee-wee behind a bush or when he had forgotten himself and stayed resting on his belly, bouncing up and down, his behind naked, while they dried out his pants. Lucien felt some comfort thinking about Guigard: tomorrow he would tell him: "I slept with Maud, she's a sweet little kid, old man, it's in her blood." But he was uncomfortable, and felt naked in the dusty heat of the metro, naked beneath a thin film of clothing, stiff and naked beside a priest, across from two mature women, like a great, soiled beanpole.

Guigard congratulated him vehemently. He was getting a little tired of Fanny. "She really has a rotten temper. Yesterday she gave me dirty looks all evening." They both agreed: there have to be women like that, because, after all, you couldn't stay chaste until you got married and then they weren't in love and they weren't sick but it would be a mistake to get attached to them. Guigard spoke of real girls with delicacy and Lucien asked him news of his sister. "She's fine," said Guigard. "She says you're a quitter. You know," he added, with a little abandon, "I'm not sorry I have a sister: you find out things you never could imagine." Lucien understood him perfectly. As a result they spoke often of girls and felt full of poetry and Guigard loved to recite the words of one of his uncles who had had much success with women: "Possibly I haven't always done the right thing in my dog's life, but there's one thing God will witness: I'd rather cut my hands off than touch a virgin." Sometimes they went to see Pierrette, Guigard's girl friend. Lucien liked Pierrette a lot, he talked to her like a big brother, teased her a little and was grateful to her because she had not cut her hair. He was completely absorbed in his political activities; every Sunday morning he went to sell *Action Française* in front of the church in Neuilly. For more than two hours, Lucien walked up and down, his face hard. The girls coming out of mass sometimes raised beautiful frank eyes toward him; then Lucien relaxed a little and felt pure and strong; he smiled at them. He explained to the gang that he respected women and he was glad to find in them the understanding he had hoped for. Besides, they almost all had sisters.

On the 17th of April, the Guigards gave a dance for Pierrette's 18th birthday and naturally Lucien was invited. He was already quite good friends with Pierrette, she called him her dancing partner and he suspected her of being a little bit in love with him. Mme. Guigard had brought in a caterer and the afternoon promised to be quite gay. Lucien danced with Pierrette several times, then went to see Guigard who was receiving his friends in the smoking room. "Hello," Guigard said, "I think you all know each other: Fleurier, Simon, Vanusse, Ledoux." While Guigard was naming his friends, Lucien saw a tall young man with red, curled hair, milky skin and hard black eyelashes, approaching them hesitantly and he was overcome with rage. "What's this fellow doing here," he wondered, "Guigard knows I can't stand Jews!" He spun on his heels and withdrew rapidly to avoid introduction. "Who is that Jew?" he asked Pierrette a moment later. "It's Weill, he's at the Hautes Etudes Commerciales; my brother met him in fencing class." "I hate Jews," Lucien said. Pierette gave a little laugh. "This one's a pretty good chap," she said. "Take me in to the buffet." Lucien drank a glass of champagne and only had time to set it down when he found himself nose to nose with Guigard and Weill. He glared at Guigard and turned his back, but Pierrette took his arm and Guigard approached him openly: "My friend Fleurier, my friend Weill," he said easily, "there, you're introduced." Weill put out his hand and Lucien felt miserable. Luckily, he suddenly remembered Desperreau: "Fleurier would have chucked the Jew in the water for good." He thrust his hands in his pockets, turned his back on Guigard and walked away. "I can never set foot in this house again," he thought, getting his coat. He felt a bitter pride. "That's what you call keeping your ideals; you can't live in society any more." Once in the street his pride melted and Lucien grew worried. "Guigard must be furious!" He shook his head and tried to tell himself with conviction, "He didn't have the right to invite a Jew if he invited me!" But his rage had left him; he saw the surprised face of Weill again with discomfort, his outstretched hand, and he felt he wanted a reconciliation: "Pierrette surely thinks I'm a heel. I should have shaken hands with him. After all, it didn't involve me in anything. Say hello to him and afterwards go right away: that's what I should have done." He wondered if he had time to go back to Guigard's. He would go up to Weill and say, "Excuse me, I wasn't feeling well." He would shake hands and say a few nice words. No. It was too late, his action was irreparable He thought with irritation, "Why did I need to show my opinions to people who can't understand them." He shrugged his shoulders nervously: it was a disaster. At that very instant Guigard and Pierrette were commenting on his behavior, Guigard was saying, "He's completely crazy!" Lucien clenched his fists. "Oh God," he thought, "how I hate them! God how I hate Jews!" and he tried to draw strength from the contemplation of this immense hatred. But it melted away under his look, in vain he thought of Leon Blum who got money from Germany and hated the French, he felt nothing more than a dismal indifference. Lucien was lucky to find Maud home. He told her he loved her and possessed her several times with a sort of rage. "It's all screwed up," he told himself, "I'll never be *anybody*." "No, no," Maud said, "stop that, my big darling, it's forbidden!" But at last she let herself go: Lucien wanted to kiss her everywhere. He felt childish and perverse; he wanted to cry.

At school, next morning, Lucien's heart tightened when he saw Guigard. Guigard looked sly and pretended not to see him. Lucien was so enraged that he could not take notes: "The bastard," he thought, "the bastard!" At the end of the class, Guigard came up to him, he was pale. "If he says a word," thought Lucien, "I'll knock his teeth in." They stayed side by side for an instant, each looking at the toes of their shoes. Finally, Guigard said in an injured voice, "Excuse me, old man, I shouldn't have done that to you." Lucien started and looked at him with distrust. But Guigard went on painfully, "I met him in the class, you see, so I thought . . . we fenced together and he invited me over to his place, but I understand, you know, I shouldn't have . . . I don't know how it happened, but when I wrote the invitations I didn't think for a second. . . ." Lucien still said nothing because the words would not come out, but he felt indulgent. Guigard, his head bowed, added, "Well, what a boner. . . ." "You big hunk of baloney!" Lucien said, slapping his shoulder, "of course I know you didn't do it on purpose." He said generously, "I was wrong, too. I acted like a heel. But what do you expect—it's stronger than I am. I can't stand them—it's physical. I feel as though they had scales on their hands. What did Pierrette say?" "She laughed like mad," Guigard said pitifully. "And the guy?" "He caught on. I said what I could, but he took off fifteen minutes later." Still humble, he added, "My parents say you were right and you couldn't have done otherwise because of your convictions." Lucien savored the word "convictions"; he wanted to hug Guigard: "It's nothing, old man," he told him; "It's nothing because we're still friends." He walked down the Boulevard Saint-Michel in a state of extraordinary exaltation: he seemed to be himself no longer.

140

He told himself, "It's funny, it isn't *me* any more. I don't recognize myself!" It was hot and pleasant; people strolled by, wearing the first astonished smile of springtime on their faces; Lucien thrust himself into this soft crowd like a steel wedge; he thought, "It's not me any more. Only yesterday I was a big, bloated bug like the crickets in Férolles." Now Lucien felt clean and sharp as a chronometer. He went into *La Source* and ordered a pernod. The gang didn't hang around the Source because the place swarmed with dagos; but dagos and Jews did not disturb Lucien that day. He felt unusual and threatening in the midst of these olive-tinted bodies which rustled like a field of oats in the wind; a monstrous clock leaning on the bar, shining red. He recognized with amusement a little Jew the J. P. had roughed up last semester in the Faculté de Droit corridors. The fat and pensive little monster had not kept the mark of the blows, he must have stayed laid up for a while and then regained his round shape; but there was a sort of obscene resignation in him.

He was happy for the time being: he yawned voluptuously; a ray of sunlight tickled his nostrils; he scratched his nose and smiled. Was it a smile? Or rather a little oscillation which had been born on the outside, somewhere in a corner of the place and which had come to die on his mouth? All the dagos were floating in dark, heavy water whose eddies jolted their flabby flesh, raised their arms, agitated their fingers and played a little with their lips. Poor bastards! Lucien almost pitied them. What did they come to France for? What sea currents had brought them and deposited them here? They could dress in clothes from tailors on the Boulevard Saint-Michel in vain; they were hardly more than jellyfish, Lucien thought, he was not a jellyfish, he did not belong to that humiliated race, he told himself, "I'm a diver." Then he suddenly forgot the Source and the dagos, he only saw a back, a wide back hunched with muscles going farther and farther away, losing itself, implacable, in the fog. He saw Guigard: Guigard was pale, he followed the back with his eyes and said to an invisible Pierrette, "Well, what a boner . . . !" Lucien was flooded with an almost intolerable joy: this powerful, solitary back was *his own!* And the scene happened yesterday! For an instant, at the cost of a violent effort, he was Guigard, he saw the humility of Guigard and felt himself deliciously terrified. "Let that be a lesson to them!" he thought. The scene changed: it was Pierrette's boudoir, it was happening in the future, Pierrette and Guigard were pointing out a name on the list of invitations.

Lucien was saying, "Oh no! Not that one! That would be fine for Lucien. Lucien can't stand Jews." Lucien studied himself once more; he thought, "I am Lucien! Somebody who can't stand Jews." He had often pronounced this sentence but today was unlike all other times. Not at all them. Of course, it was apparently a simple statement, as if someone had said, "Lucien doesn't like oysters," or, "Lucien likes to dance." But there was no mistaking it: love of dancing might be found in some little Jew who counted no more than a fly: all you had to do was look at that damned kike to know that his likes and dislikes clung to him like his odor, like the reflections of his skin, that they disappeared with him like the blinking of his heavy eyelids, like his sticky, voluptuous smiles. But Lucien's anti-semitism was of a different sort: unrelenting and pure, it stuck out of him like a steel blade menacing other breasts. "It's . . . sacred," he thought. He remembered his mother when he was little, sometimes speaking to him in a certain special tone of voice: "Papa is working in his office." This sentence seemed a sacramental formula to him which suddenly conferred a halo of religious obligations on him, such as not playing with his air gun and not shouting "Tararaboom!"; he walked down the hall on tiptoe as if he were in a cathedral. "Now it's my turn," he thought with satisfaction. Lowering their voices, they said, "Lucien doesn't like Jews," and people would feel paralyzed, their limbs transfixed by a swarm of aching little arrows. "Guigard and Pierrette," he said tenderly, "are children." They had been guilty but it sufficed for Lucien to show his teeth and they were filled with remorse, they had spoken in a low voice and walked on tiptoe.

Lucien felt full of self-respect for the second time. But this time he no longer needed the eyes of Guigard: he appeared respectable in his own eyes—in his own eyes which had finally pierced his envelope of flesh, of likes and dislikes, habits and humors. "Where I sought myself," he thought, "I could not find myself." In good faith he took a detailed counting of all he *was*. "But if I could only be what I am I wouldn't be worth any more than that little kike." What could one discover searching in this mucous intimacy if not the sorrow of flesh, the ignoble lie of equality and disorder? "First maxim," Lucien said, "not to try and see inside yourself; there is no mistake more dangerous." The real Lucien—he knew now—had to be sought in the eyes of others, in the frightened obedience of Pierrette and Guigard, the hopeful waiting of all those beings who grew and ripened for him, these young apprentice girls who would become *his* workers, people of Férolles, great and small, of whom he would one day be the master. Lucien was almost afraid, he felt almost too great for himself. So many people were waiting for him, at attention: and he was and always would be this immense waiting of others. "That's a leader," he thought. And he saw a hunched, muscular back re-appear, then, immediately afterwards, a cathedral. He was inside, walking on tiptoe beneath the sifted light that fell from the windows. "Only this time I am the cathedral!" He stared intently at his neighbor, a tall Cuban, brown and mild as a cigar. He must absolutely find words to express this extraordinary discovery. Quietly, cautiously, he raised his hand to his forehead, like a lighted candle, then drew into himself for an instant, thoughtful and holy, and the words came of themselves. "I HAVE RIGHTS!" Rights! Something like triangles and circles: it was so perfect that it didn't exist, you could trace thousands of circles with a compass in vain, you could never make a single circle. Generations of workers could even scrupulously obey the commands of Lucien, they would never exhaust his right to command, rights were beyond existence, like mathematical objects and religious dogma. And now Lucien was just that: an enormous bouquet of responsibilities and rights. He had believed that he existed by chance for a long time, but it was due to a lack of sufficient thought. His place in the sun was marked in Férolles long before his birth. They were *waiting* for him long before his father's marriage: if he had come into the world it was to occupy that place: "I exist," he thought, "because I have the right to exist." And, perhaps for the first time, he had a flashing, glorious vision of his destiny. Sooner or later he would go to the Centrale (it made no difference). Then he would drop Maud (she always wanted to sleep with him, it was tiresome; their confused flesh giving off an odor of scorched rabbit stew in the torrid heat of springtime. "And then, Maud belongs to everybody. Today me, tomorrow somebody else, none of it makes any sense"); he would go and live in Férolles. Somewhere in France there was a bright young girl like Pierrette, a country girl with eyes like flowers who would stay chaste for him: sometimes she tried to imagine her future master, this gentle and terrible man; but she could not. She was a virgin; in the most secret part of her body she recognized the right of Lucien alone to possess her. He would marry her, she would be *his* wife, the tenderest of his rights. When, in the evening, she would undress with slender, sacred gestures, it would be like a holocaust. He would take her in his arms with the approval of everyone, and tell her, "You belong to me!" What she would show him she would have the right to show to him alone and for him the act of love would be a voluptuous counting of his goods. His most tender right, his most intimate right: the right to be respected to the very flesh, obeyed to the very bed. "I'll marry young," he thought. He thought too that he would like to have many children; then he thought of his father's work; he was impatient to continue it and wondered if M. Fleurier was not going to die soon.

A clock struck noon; Lucien rose. The metamorphosis was complete: a graceful, uncertain adolescent had entered this café one hour earlier; now a man left, a leader among Frenchmen. Lucien took a few steps in the glorious light of a French morning. At the corner of Rue des Écoles and the Boulevard Saint-Michel he went towards a stationery shop and looked at himself in the mirror: he would have liked to find on his own face the impenetrable look he admired on Lemordant's. But the mirror only reflected a pretty, headstrong little face that was not yet terrible. "I'll grow a moustache," he decided.

New Directions Paperbooks—A Partial Listing

For a complete listing request free catalog from
New Directions, 80 Eighth Avenue, New York 10011

†Bilingual

For a complete listing request free catalog from
New Directions, 80 Eighth Avenue, New York 10011   †Bilingual